The Adventures of
Tobio
in the Land of the Fays

The Adventures of
Tobio
in the Land of the Fays

by
Hélène Gisiger

translated by
Michael Shreve

A Black Coat Press Book

Visit our website at www.blackcoatpress.com

ISBN 978-1-64932-411-5. First Printing: September 2025.
Published by Black Coat Press, an imprint of Hollywood Comics.com, 18321 Ventura Blvd. Suite 915, Tarzana, CA 91356.

TABLE OF CONTENTS

Introduction

Hélène Gisiger is the author of five children's books: the three featuring Tobio collected in this volume, plus two more:

Les Aventures du Vieux Nain Fuit-Fuit (1943)
Les Trésors du Nain Rap (1948)

All were initially published in Switzerland in the 1940s, leading us to assume that she was Swiss.

There is no information about her, either at the French Bibliothèque Nationale, nor at the Swiss Bibliothèque Nationale. Her then-publisher, the Editions de la Baconnière in Neuchâtel, when contacted, had no information about her either—at least not easily accessed. (They might have had some in dusty old archives, assuming they have kept any, but understandably, they did not volunteer to search them.) And as Gisiger's books are no longer in print, there is no way to track down the author, or more likely her heirs, through conventional means.

Genealogy sites identified three women who might be likely candidates, but lacking any supporting information, it is impossible to tell if any of them was the author of these books.

It is always perilous to draw too many conclusions about a writer based solely on his or her works. Nevertheless, in this case, based on the morality and symbolic contents of *Tobio*, plus the fact that the eponymous hero is a boy-scout, we may safely assume that Gisiger was a Christian.

It is unlikely that Gisiger had read a copy of Marie-Anne de Roumier-Robert's *Voyage de Milord Céton dans les Sept Planètes* (1766)[1] but even though *Tobio* was penned 175 years later, it presents some remarkable similarities with it. In the former, Lord Seaton and his sister Monime travel to the seven planets (as were then known) of the Solar System on the wings of a great sprite named Zachiel. On each world, they experience what might be dubbed a "morality play," a thinly disguised way for the author to comment upon her times. Cleary, Tobio was meant to be first an entertaining children's book, but occasionally Gisiger does not shy from commenting on her own times (see her own view on education in Book 1), while, at the same time, trying to teach children morals.

Perhaps the fact that astronomer Rupert Wildt identified absorption bands of ammonia and methane in the spectra of Jupiter in 1932 was not known to Gisiger? Unlike Madame de Roumier-Robert, she could not be ignorant of the fact that the planet was a gas giant, a totally unsuitable location for her "Land of the Fays." Why not choose a Narnia-like land like C. S. Lewis did at about the same time, rather than Jupiter?[2]

Perhaps the reason is to be found in the conservative forces that equated science with Darwinism in France at the time, which believed that the Heavens should be inhabited by angels, not aliens, as was claimed in the 1930s in an attack by the same thinkers against Maurice Renard's classic SF novel *Le Péril Bleu* (1911)?[3]

---

[1] Available as *The Voyages of Lord Seaton to the Seven Planets*, Black Coat Press, ISBN 978-1-61227-446-1.

[2] Lewis originally conceived Narnia in 1939 but did not finish writing the first book *The Lion, the Witch and the Wardrobe* until 1949.

[3] Available as *The Blue Peril*, Black Coat Press, ISBN 978-1-935558-17-0.

In any event, there are indeed similarities between Gisiger's Jupiter and Lewis' Narnia: their richly-developed geography, fauna and flora, their mythical creatures and, yes, even their Christian symbolism all strike a similar chord.

Was Gisiger possibly influenced by *The Wizard of Oz*? Unlikely. The MGM film was not released in France, Belgium and Switzerland until 1946. Baum's novel had been translated in 1931, but its sequels, expanding on the rich universe of Oz, were not translated until the 1980s. It is more likely that she was influenced by Walt Disney's animated classic *Snow White* first released in France in 1938.

Halfway between *The Chronicles of Narnia* and *The Wizard of Oz*, *The Adventures of Tobio in the Land of the Fays* remains a forgotten classic of children's fantasy literature today, well deserving of greatest recognition.

Jean-Marc Lofficier

HÉLÈNE GISIGER

TOBIO
SES AVENTURES
AU PAYS DES FÉES

A NEUCHATEL
AUX ÉDITIONS DE LA BACONNIÈRE

THE ADVENTURES OF TOBIO IN THE LAND OF THE FAYS

CHAPTER I
Tobio Discovers the Land of the Fays

Tobio made a discovery. In the evening, at the hour when day fades to twilight, just before the tiny, curious eyes of the stars appear, he noticed that a huge, downy wing was sweeping over the ground. He saw it coming, huge, light, from the horizon still rosy from the sunset. It caressed the dark and proud pine trees that scented the air pleasantly; it closed the eyes of the little flowers; it carried dreams into the hearts of men.

Tobio, at twelve years-old, was not just a dreamer; he also liked to do things and knew how to think. He had to get hold of this wing to see where it was going. He took all afternoon to get ready. He put on his scout's uniform, stuffed his pockets with food and string and didn't forget his army knife and flashlight.

When the last rays of the sun had gone to join their brothers, he climbed to the top of the pine tree in the garden and waited.

The big wing appeared in the distance, bringing the velvet night. As it got closer a cozy breeze arose.

Go! A big jump! Tobio grabbed a clump of pearly white feathers and lay down snugly on the wing. Near him was a man with a kind and thoughtful face watching the stars.

Farther away was an old man loaded with instruments who shouted, "Magnificent! We'll be there in an hour."

"Where?" Tobio asked.

"What a question! Where else but the planet Mars! Oh, my friends, what an experience! Magnificent! Magnificent!"

Tobio didn't have time to answer because a huge ball appeared, enclosed in pale light. As they got closer, they saw milky lakes shimmering, a ring of mountains and valleys shrouded in mists. Tobio even thought he could see the shapes of winged women moving slowly.

Oops! Tobio almost lost his balance. The man next to him had just jumped to the ground. But their weird chariot kept going since it hadn't yet reached its goal.

"Where did that man go?" Tobio asked.

"That poet? On the Moon. To the Muses!"

"Oh, this is really the Moon? What are the Muses?"

"Those winged creatures you saw. They're elusive and impulsive. Poor fool! But what that is, I really have no idea. Look."

They were approaching a land shining with a light so bright that it was impossible to see anything. The old man nervously went through his pockets and his bags searching for a pair of blue glasses. But they were far past it when he found them carelessly wrapped up with a sandwich.

He was sorely disappointed and groaned, "Ah, missing Mercury like that, unacceptable!"

It took Venus coming into view, so huge that they soon couldn't see its edges, to make him forget about the mishap.

Scented and sonorous vapors arose from the planet. Tobio and his companion stretched out, suddenly steeped in happiness. They closed their eyes, drunk on joy, thinking of nothing but living in the present moment, hoping that it would last forever.

Little by little the vapors faded away. Venus disappeared and the two travelers looked at each other in a daze, wondering if they had dreamed.

"What a strange route," the scientist said. "I'm realizing that the wing is going in big circles. We should have reached Mars a long time ago. I thought it would be our first stop. Unless we missed it!"

But soon the two were flooded with a warm, velvety light. Nearby, like a gigantic ruby, a star was shining. The wing approached it slowly, but was soon skimming over the top of a mountain.

"Oh, look, red trees, red grass and red rocks. Where are we?"

Tobio didn't get an answer. With all his tools and instruments, the old man had disappeared. His excited voice echoed from afar, "Magnificent! Magnificent!"

Tobio was so tired that he fell asleep. He dreamed of dragons, of fantastical beings. A little, devilish fellow came close to him and tried to throw fire in his eyes. Tobio woke up screaming. He was in a starry bath. As far as the eye could see, it was clouded with golden dots. Big ones, little ones, spinning and dancing like motes of dust, huge ones in a ray of sunlight. It lasted two hours, then the wing entered a dark blue space that became brighter and brighter.

Tobio leaned over and noticed that he was above a world where he could see nothing but a thick, cottony blanket of intense blue. Because he was leaning over carelessly he lost his balance and fell head first through the blue fluff.

Tobio thought he was lying under his favorite linden tree because he smelled the rascally grass that was tickling his ears. He didn't dare move for fear of disturbing the bird that was singing such a marvelous song. He'd never heard such a voice. It was certainly a nightingale. Tomorrow he'd be sure to tell his teacher. But he had to see the singer.

Slowly he opened his eyes and then his mouth. He was indeed near a tree with big, delicately serrated leaves and at the end of the branches hung odd, pink, heart-shaped fruit. A bright red baby bird with a blue head was pecking at one. Tobio sat and gasped an astonished, "Oh!"

He was in a prairie sprinkled with clumps of trees. The grass was thin and soft as velvet. Weird flowers were brightly colored. Three lovely ponies who were grazing looked at him curiously; a white kid goat with a wet little nose came to lick his neck. A superb lion came down a path, being teased by a young gazelle. A dark panther scampered down a tree and came to purr at his feet, half-closing its golden eyes. Animals were coming from all over, pushing and shoving each other, to get a look at him.

Tobio thought about it and soon remembered what had happened to him. So, he was in a new world! Maybe it was Paradise since the wild beasts were friends with the other animals. But it was strange that there were no humans!

Tobio decided to explore this new land. He picked a fruit to taste it. It was so good! It was like nougat, but juicy and refreshing. He put some in his pockets and walked away through all the animals asking to be petted.

After an hour's walk he came to the foot of a hill, which he climbed. Not one animal followed him. At the top he saw something so marvelous that he couldn't believe it was real.

He was looking at a splendid castle made of pink marble. A vast garden, sprinkled with small, silvery lakes reflecting bushes covered with purple flowers surrounded it. He strolled down a path of fine, pink sand. On all sides, bouquets of silky carnations scented the air, gentle streams babbled gaily and wonderful birds filled the light air with the boundless harmony of their pure voices.

When he got near the castle he heard voices. One was clear and resonant like a bell; the other was low and lovely like an organ. A cute lady with big, brown eyes and laughing lips, dressed in a long robe that looked cut from a moonbeam, was walking arm in arm with a tall, blond man who was gazing on her with tender, blue eyes. He wore a blue, silk suit with a diamond star glittering on his chest and in his right hand was a sparkling staff.

Tobio stepped forward and bowed, greeting them politely.

"Welcome to the Land of the Fays," the man responded, raising his staff.

"Before you stand the King of the Fays and the loveliest of them, the fay Câline."

"How happy I am!" Tobio cried out as he admired the gorgeous fay and the handsome king. "I got on a giant wing to see where it was going and it flew over this land but I was leaning over too far and I lost my balance."

"And now you're the guest of the King on the beautiful planet Jupiter."

"Oh, thank you. But tell me, is the whole planet inhabited by fays?"

"No, only a part. Farther to the north are the mountains, the domain of the dwarves, gnomes and all kinds of goblins. In the south, there's a high plain, full of canyons and chasms, the realm of sorcerers. Then comes the sea, the empire of the water sprites, and a group of islands on which other sprites live. The poles are the vast lands of the wizards. The South Pole has a gigantic fortress in which the Great Spirit lives. It's impossible to reach it without passing through harrowing ordeals. So far, only one man has ever succeeded—the sorcerer Sirius, my best friend. He's incredibly strong, brave and smart. The North Pole is home to the Supreme Being, whom no one has ever seen but about whom they tell fantastic tales.

"My realm is separated from its neighbors by three magic circles that no one can cross without my permission. But it's open to the land of sorcerers, who are friends of the fays. You'll be able to visit it and learn things so that, if you really want to, you can explore the whole planet without too much danger. But night is falling. Look over there, that blue star, that's Earth."

Very touched, Tobio contemplated the small dot of light that held so many people and all the things that he loved.

A huge crescent moon rose up from the horizon and reached the middle of the sky, casting a soft light over Jupiter. At its zenith, the splendid orb, encircled by two colorful rings, sent forth its multicolored beams. The lakes changed into opals, the flowers turned orange and blue—it was a real fairy-tales land.

A soft hand touched Tobio's arm. "Come, it's time for the nectar."

After climbing a few gray marble steps, passing by rows of red roses and the magnificent fountains that decorated the entrance to the castle, Tobio was brought into the grand parlor. In the center of the room was a long table around which were bustling a bunch of marvelous creatures dressed in clothes made of fabric that looked as soft and shimmering as butterfly wings. Their shiny, curly hair was sprinkled with delicate flowers. They were all smiling and babbling as they poured a golden liquid, which smelled delicious, into glasses shaped like water lilies. Big, silver bowls full of strange, tantalizing fruit were sitting at either end of the table. In the middle were odd-shaped cookies, savory pies and velvety creams that were irresistible to greedy eyes.

When the fays saw the King, they came to dance before him. Tobio noticed one old fay with an elegant, friendly face sitting on a silky, iridescent throne. The King bowed before her and introduced Tobio.

Then he said, "This is the fay Bountiful, my mother, who is Queen of the fays."

"I love Earth children," the Queen said. "I hope you'll enjoy yourself with us. If ever you need help or advice, come find me."

At that moment they heard a bell and almost right away twenty or so men, all tall, all looking proud and intelligent, came in. Tobio took notice at once of one of them who calmly approached the King and shook his hand. Tobio thought he was quite impressive with his tanned, stern face and rugged appearance.

As the King asked the sorcerers which one would be willing to be a mentor, Tobio blushed cheerfully when his favorite volunteered.

"Well then, Tobio," said the King, "it'll be my friend Sirius who will be teaching you from now on about Jupiter. You can sit next to him at the table."

On his other side at the table Tobio saw a blond, perky fay who played all kinds of jokes. She was called Mischief, and had the cutest little nose that he'd ever seen. Another didn't stop talking the whole time, tinkling her bells every time she laughed. His mentor told him she was called Titter and was always happy and bubbly.

"Mentor, who is the nicest fay?" he asked.

"They all are, Tobio, but I'm particular fond of the wood fay Spruce. She's at the end of the table. See how beautiful she is with her dark hair and big, green eyes. If you want, you can come with me to her house tomorrow. She lives in a simple cottage in the middle of the forest where all is peace and pleasure."

"Oh, that would be wonderful, mentor. Will you take me to visit all the fays?"

"Certainly, Tobio, and all the sorcerers, too."

"Mentor, you're the best. Will you teach me how to become as handsome, brave and smart as you?"

"That'll be easy, Tobio, since you really want it."

It was only when Tobio was full and had watched everyone present for a long time that he realized the walls of the parlor were made of rosebuds and a big diamond star was lighting the room and the carpet was pink and fluttering like a swan's soft down.

Then the King and Queen stood up and announced that it was time to get some rest.

The sorcerer Sirius led his young ward to a room carpeted with daisies that were already sleeping and laid him down on a bed of soft moss that smelled of violets.

"Good night, Tobio. I'll come get you tomorrow."

"Good night, mentor, and thank you very much, very very much…"

Tobio had fallen asleep.

CHAPTER II
Zalou's abduction

All the daisies were quivering, cracking open their eyes and smiling at Tobio as he woke up. Big, colorful butterflies were caressing his hair with their velvety wings. In a corner, a waterfall suddenly sprang out, fresh and cheerful. That was all it took for Tobio to be on his feet and ready to go. With its tinkling laughter the waterfall filled a big, white marble pool. Tobio jumped in merrily.

"Hello! Hello! Are you ready?"

The sorcerer Sirius was there, watching his ward amiably.

"Oh, hello, mentor, am I late?"

"Not too much. The dew's already been served, but we left your place."

"What's the dew?"

"The dew, child, is the first meal of the day. It's served when the flames of the Sun appear on the horizon. It's basically made up of refreshing and nutritious dishes like plant sap, fruit juice and *kalilou*, a kind of vegetable that tastes like your earthly beefsteaks. But come on and have a taste."

Tobio followed his mentor into the garden where, in the shade of flowering trees, before the curious gaze of the golden fish in the pond, he enjoyed feasting like a glutton.

"Well, well, I guess you find the dew to your liking. Good. Now let's get going."

At the garden gate a big surprise was in store for Tobio. A long, jointed caterpillar with big, red eyes and bristling with iron spikes was waiting there. By pulling a small lever, the sorcerer opened the vehicle's top to reveal a row of six comfortable armchairs. Sirius got behind the wheel and examined the dashboard full of buttons. Since this machine was extremely interesting to Tobio, his mentor told him all about it.

"My sectaphore can travel on land, on the sea and in the air. I built it myself and am the only one on the planet to have a machine like this. When I travel in the Land of the Fays, or in my own, I leave the top down, but in dangerous lands, I close it up and fill the spikes with fluid by pressing the three buttons in the middle. The eyes are headlights for nighttime. They move freely."

"But, mentor, what do you use for gas?"

"That product doesn't exist here; it's too smelly. Moreover, it's very annoying because the tank's always getting empty, you have to stop to fill it up, you lose time, and you get dirty; no, it's really too primitive. I use solar energy. I capture a kind of ray from the sun with a device that's installed in between the eyes. The air is full of this energy, so why not use it? On Earth, you have something like it—you call it electricity, I think. But solar energy is better because it's a lot more powerful and it isn't dangerous to work with. We can capture it directly without having to build all those factories and machines. Now let's go. We'll go slowly and keep on land so you can admire the countryside."

Gently, softly, like a giant snake, the vehicle slithered over the flowery grass, around the trees, crawled up hills and always without feeling the slightest bump inside.

Since Tobio was astonished, his mentor explained to him that the bottom of the sectaphore was equipped with thousands of tiny, jointed feet that moved in different directions following the terrain and thus kept the vehicle perfect straight and stable.

Tobio saw nothing of the landscape because all his attention was concentrated on the marvelous sectaphore. So, he was really surprised when he heard rumbling and whistles and a bunch of weird noises.

"We've arrived at the fay Tintin's home. She loves children, especially from Earth. Every day she goes to pick up dozens of them from amongst the poor and unhappy. She keeps them with her until they get healthy, strong and smart."

Tobio looked out. There were children everywhere, pink and active and merry, shouting, laughing, singing. Some were playing on pretty carousels that they spun around, others were driving cars, riding bikes, in planes, etc. Never had Tobio seen so many wonderful toys.

Since he was surprised that there were no accidents, his mentor explained to him that collisions were impossible because the toys were activated by a magic fluid.

The children welcomed the sectaphore with shouts of joy and escorted it to the huge, leafy castle where the fay Tintin, tiny, pink and chubby, offered them a delicious lemonade with a smile. Nearby, children were frolicking on the shores of a charming lake, others were rowing zealously in the water, and some were racing on rubber seahorses.

But Sirius was in a hurry. The travelers soon bid farewell to the sweet fay who invited Tobio to come and spend his vacation with her.

The sectaphore went down a path going through the woods and arrived at the foot of a small mountain that it had a hard time climbing.

Almost at the top, on the southern slope, surrounded by giant pine trees, was the cottage of the fay Spruce. It was all made of brown wood, with a roof covered with fresh rhododendrons. Ornate galleries across the front of the house emerged from clumps of bellflowers that shook their fragile bells in the light breeze, sounding like rustling silk. In the front was a carpet of gentian, little blue eyes, bold and eager, or big horns, deeper blue and more mysterious, with black flecks that blossomed into stars.

Tobio told his mentor to stay on the path for fear of crushing his favorite flowers. Silky edelweiss decorated the entrance to the cottage along with lilies of the valley and sweet violets that hid shyly under the foliage, revealing their presence by their enchanting scent.

When Tobio and his mentor got out of the sectaphore, the front door opened and a tall, slender fay with milk-white skin, shiny black curls and big green eyes came walking gracefully toward them. How happy the sorcerer Sirius looked!

"Pretty Spruce, I'd like to introduce you to my ward, Tobio."

"Glad to meet you, Tobio. I hope we'll become good friends. Would you like to play with my squirrels while I finish preparing the welcome?"

Tobio looked questioningly at his mentor who explained, "The welcome is the meal we eat in the middle of the day with every visitor who comes to our land. I'll also say that it's excellent, especially here at the Spruce's home. Enjoy yourself. Go and find the squirrels. They're usually hanging out around that grove of trees over there on the left."

Tobio turned around and looked astonished at his mentor because the sectaphore was moving. Dozens of arms with brushes were scrubbing away and polishing the machine.

"An impressive system, isn't it, my boy? We need to think of things like this because there are no servants in the Land of the Fays. We're all equal and we do out best to help each other out. All the cleaning is done automatically because no one likes this kind of work. When I designed my machine, I had to think of this. When I got out, I pressed a button that started the cleaning system, which will take exactly fifteen minutes to do the job. Look, it's already done."

Indeed, the arms were folding back inside and the sectaphore sat gleaming in the sun. Tobio went in search of the squirrels.

There were ten, twenty of them, lively, playful, scampering around on the low branches. All of a sudden, plop! One of them jumped onto Tobio's shoulder. It climbed into his hair while another started clambered up his leg. At first Tobio was annoyed, then he got angry. The filthy beasts, how dare they! Wham, a little slap here, another there.

"That'll teach you some manners. Who would have a mind to sit on someone's head!"

Pouting, the squirrels went back to their trees and bombarded him with pine cones. Tobio turned his back on them and went back to the cottage since his stomach was grumbling loudly for the welcome.

Spruce, Tobio and his mentor were finishing up the succulent meal when a strange contraption showed up. It was a kind of chariot, shaped like a round bowl, sitting on six big wheels and pulled by three ostriches. Inside was a black armchair with red polka dots on which sat a funny-looking man, no taller than Tobio, thin as a twig, with weird, silvery, round eyes, pointy ears and a lipless mouth that stretched from ear to ear. He was dressed in yellow from head to toe.

The little man shot out of the chariot and loudly, excitedly shouted, "Good fay, come quick, my benefactress has disappeared!"

"Come now, Tati, sit down," Sirius said, "and tell us everything calmly. Maybe there's no reason to worry yourself. You know how the fay Zalou can be pretty eccentric. She probably got the crazy idea to go somewhere and, as always, she left on a whim and forgot to tell you."

"Oh, no, she'd never leave without taking her talisman. It was left on her bed! Plus, her parrots are screeching up a storm. I can't calm them down. I'm sure something's happened to my good fay."

Sirius listened to Tati. A crease formed between his eyebrows. He was back to his former cold and serious self.

"Let's go and see," he said. "You're coming, aren't you, Spruce? Tati, untie your ostriches and get into my sectaphore—it'll be faster."

After quickly crossing through Spruce's country, the travelers got to the domain of the fay Zalou. The whole valley was just a vast garden that was an unforgettable sight. Everywhere were big, square flowerbeds, pink, red and black, separated by groves of trees or lovely gazebos. In the middle of the valley, on a hill covered in red flowers, stood a castle of black marble, flanked by four elegant towers. The lozenge-shaped windows glinted gold and the door was like a flaming rose. The interior of the castle was weird, asymmetrical, nooks and crannies everywhere in which were the most unexpected things: a fountain, an aviary, a mossy bed, a purple satin seat, etc.

Sirius and his companions headed straight for the private rooms of the fay. They first entered a round room in the middle of which was a fountain of gurgling water in a pond with splendid, brightly colored fish playing hide-and-seek among the water lilies. A long couch with thick white fur stretched along the walls. Next to a window hung a dark curtain hiding the door to the bedroom. There,

Tobio first noticed a portrait of a very thin, tall woman with golden skin, a young, mischievous face and silver hair. She was oddly dressed in a clingy fabric that looked like snakeskin. Tobio thought that Zalou was definitely weird but nice.

The sorcerer was standing by the soft bed staring at a huge ruby, so shiny and pure that Tobio was dazed. It was the famous talisman of the fay who, until today, had never been separated from it. All of a sudden Sirius bent down and picked up two gray feathers that he examined closely. Spruce, Tobio and Tati watched him anxiously. They could hear the noisy shrieks of the parrots nearby.

"My friends," the sorcerer said, "I believe I've found the truth. Look at these two feathers and tell me what you think."

Spruce blurted out, "They must belong to a big bird but certainly not to Zalou's parrots. Besides them there are finches, budgies, nightingales and the cuckoos I gave her recently. So, I don't see where these feathers could have come from."

Tobio was really good in natural history. One look was all it took for him to identify them.

"Mentor, I don't have any doubt that these are eagle feathers."

"Bravo, Tobio, you're going to be someone special! Indeed, these are eagle feathers. Do you know what I'm thinking? No? Well, you all know that there are no eagles in the Land of the Fays, but I know a sorcerer who has this animal as an emblem and he's got a lot of them. He only travels in a carriage pulled by his eagles. His name is Truko, the red-eyed wizard with suction cups on his arms. Tati, take Spruce and Tobio to the King of the Fays. They'll explain the situation. As for me, I'm going straight back to the land of sorcerers."

"Mentor, please, bring me with you! I'm not scared of anything and I can be helpful."

"Very well, my boy, but we won't leave until tonight because I'd like to teach you to drive my sectaphore first. That way, in case of great danger you'll still be able to save yourself."

"Dear Sirius," Spruce said, "be careful. I'd be so unhappy if anything happened to you!"

"Don't fear, beautiful fay, I will be careful and I will succeed in order to gaze into your gentle eyes again. Within ten days I'll bring back your friend along with a souvenir of Truko. Besides, I have an assistant now. He'll be invaluable, I'm sure of it."

Tobio blushed as his heart beat frantically.

CHAPTER III
The red-eyed wizard

For two hours already the sorcerer had been revealing all the secrets of his vehicle to his companion. Tobio was still not an expert driver but, if need be, he could drive without too much risk. He realized the expedition was so serious that he asked his mentor to teach him Morse code with hands and a flashlight like the sorcerers learned. That way, if they happened to get separated, they would still have a way to communicate.

"Bravo, Tobio," the sorcerer beamed, "you really are a partner full of surprises!"

But Spruce, who wanted to be there when they left, together with Tati, had prepared nectar and some delicious food for their journey, all of which was quickly put away in a hermetically sealed space in the back of the sectaphore.

It was almost midnight when the two friends hit the road.

"You can sleep, Tobio. It's nighttime so you won't see anything. Moreover, we'll be cruising at 3000 feet altitude to get there as fast as possible. So, it'll take 36 hours at most to reach the land of wizards."

With all its feet retracted, the sectaphore propelled its polished hull through the air. They barely noticed the faint whistling as it went. Tobio dozed off…

It was the smell of a savory pie that his mentor was slicing that woke him up. The sun was shining on a deep blue sea. Here and there, mountainous islands sparkled like silver. Tobio was enthralled.

"Oh, mentor, is that the sea?"

"Of course. Did you have nice dreams? Let's eat."

"Mentor, this is the first time I've seen the sea. In my country there are only mountains, rivers and lakes. I would never have believed it could be so big and so blue. And those islands, what are they made of that they sparkle like that?"

"They're limestone mountains and it's the reflection of the sun that makes them look silver. But what do you think of this pie and the drink? Spruce spoiled us."

"Fabulous! I'm starving!"

A big, green island appeared.

"Look, Tobio, we're about to pass over the domain of the sprite Oax. His wonderful castle is built of shells. We'll have to pay him a visit next month. Oh, but I really think I need some rest. Would you take my place at the wheel? We're headed in the right direction, southwest, make sure we keep to it. If anything goes wrong, wake me up."

Tobio drove for hours. His mentor would have been proud of him. Just the thought of this made him so happy that he wanted to skip and jump around like a young colt. He was starting to get used to the sea and its immensity. He even started to think there was no more land when the horizon suddenly looked like it was lined with a great, dark cloud. They got closer—big, forested mountains came into view.

"Mentor, mentor, where are we?"

"Good grapes, how could I have slept so long! We're already at the Great Wind Mountains that surround the Land of Red Dwarves. You're an ace, Tobio, and a smart boy. In an hour we'll reach our goal and it'll be completely dark."

"That's weird, mentor, because it's only noon."

"True, my boy, noon here, but it's midnight over there. Don't forget that we're on the other side of the globe. Look at that mountain that's taller than the others. That's the home of the Dwarf King. It's crowned with a crystal ball that reflects on a mirror inside the castle an image of what's outside the castle for half a mile around. But there's the entrance to the kingdom of wizards. I'm going to turn off the sectaphore's eyes, close the top and fill the spikes with fluid. Better to take precautions in a land like this."

Dimly lit by the moon, Tobio watched the country unrolling beneath him. It was a vast plain with many hills. On one of them was a huge, dark building looming over the land. At the very top of a tower, two red balls were glowing.

"Darn!" the sorcerer said. "there's nothing we can do! The wizard is awake. See his eyes shining in the night like lanterns? Ah, my dear friend Truko must be a little worried tonight. We'll go back to the dwarves and return at dawn."

The crystal ball must have seen them because, despite the late hour, the door of the royal mountain was open when they got there and two rows of dwarves lined the path for them all the way into a room that was so huge and so high that it took their breath away. There were hundreds of galleries and balconies swarming with the little people with red skin and amusing faces full of mischief and mirth. Bunches of pointy hats were scurrying hither and thither.

Tobio was pulled by his mentor in front of the marvelously carved, ruby throne at the top of a hundred tiny steps. On it was perched a pudgy little red man dressed in bright blue. He wore a sapphire crown and his fingernails and teeth were painted blue.

"Greetings to my great friend Sirius and his companion," he said.

Then he hit a gong on his left and ordered, "Bring the welcome."

Almost immediately a table full of bowls and red platters piled with various mushrooms, pine cone cakes, acorn and hazelnut pies were placed before them.

Tobio and the sorcerer ate while the gabby king told them everything that had happened in his realm since Sirius' last visit. All the dwarves, like a flock of curious sparrows, were there listening and watching. The two guests just nodded their heads because it was hard to get a word in edgewise when the king was talking!

Soon Tobio was straining to keep his eyes open. His eyelids were getting heavier and heavier, so heavy…

"Get up, Tobio, it's time to leave, the sun's about to rise."

Surprised, Tobio sat up on his bed of moss.

"Well, yes, my boy, I put you to bed like a big baby. You slept like an angel. Quick, we'll eat on the way. The Dwarf King, Kyxy, was kind enough to pack up the dew for us. When I told him the purpose of our expedition, he offered to camouflage my sectaphore so it'll go unnoticed by the big eagle eyes that keep watch on the top of the towers. Come and see what it looks like now."

From the doorway Tobio couldn't see the machine, just a row of overgrown bushes. He burst out laughing and shouted, "Long live King Kyxy and his cleverness!"

But the pudgy king was sleeping soundly and his subjects, except for the three sentinels at the mirror, were following him into dreamland with their little fists closed, their noses wrinkled and their mouths open.

A row of bushes dashed through the forest to the amazement of the chipper squirrels, the curious magpies and the old crows. They'd be talking about it for days to come.

"Mentor, I have an idea. You stay in the sectaphore when we get to the castle and I'll go introduce myself to the red wizard. He doesn't know me and won't be suspicious. I'll try to keep him busy so you can do whatever you have to."

Sirius looked at Tobio with admiration. "Better and better, my boy, in a year you'll be showing me what's what. We'll follow your plan. Take this whistle and if you're ever in danger, blow and I'll come running."

As Tobio was knocking at the door to the castle, he whispered to himself, "I'm not afraid, I'm brave and strong."

Silently the door cracked open and a cold wind engulfed Tobio. Weird, winged creatures, horned, black and covered in soft hair like the wings of a bat, brushed by him, bumping and jostling him unpleasantly. In front of him was a long, smooth hallway sloping upwards. Tobio had a hard time walking because there were no banisters to hold onto and no steps. Halfway up it he slipped and fell back to the starting point.

Raucous laughter exploded. "What are you waiting for, microbe? Does somebody have to come and push you from behind?"

"Certainly not! I'm coming up right now!"

Tobio kicked off his shoes, which he hung on his belt, wet his hands like he'd seen country folk do, got down on all fours and was at the end of the hallway in a few minutes. He was looking down another hallway, lined with doors, one of which was open at the end of the passage. Tobio headed for it and stood in the doorway, astonished.

It was like a cave. There were dark holes everywhere with horrible monsters sticking out of them. In the middle of the space, sitting on a big rock, was Truko.

Tobio had figured he'd deal with the wizard like he did with mean dogs on Earth: he'd stare him down. But how could he stare into those glowing orbs? *If only I had sunglasses!* he thought. It was a funny idea that made him smile and also calmed him down.

He stepped forward, bowed formally before the wizard and said, "Greetings, oh great wizard."

He got no answer. Truko didn't move a muscle. While Tobio waited patiently, he examined the wizard's nose. It was a mother-nose out of which sprang twenty or so little ones, each more purple than the others. Since the glowing eyes burned brighter, Tobio figured that the wizard didn't appreciate the examination. So, he forgot about the nose and smiled kindly at those thick lips, the hairy, pointy ears and bristles instead of hair. All of a sudden he noticed some flabby, blackish things hanging motionless under the wizard's arms. He felt a little queasy.

Truko laughed and shook his tentacles. "You like the suctions? They'll drain out a microbe like you in less than a second!"

Tobio glanced nervously at the window and saw Sirius sneaking up to it. "Oh, Great Wizard, they're incredible, let me admire them! Imagine that I came from Earth just to see you. Over there, they tell so many fantastic stories about you. Your strength and intelligence are apparently unrivaled on the whole planet."

Truko gurgled and grumbled.

Tobio went on.

"Everyone's surprised that you're not the Wizard King. What does your king do? I've never heard of him."

Tobio's sharp ears heard a faint sound in the hallway.

Truko stood up but Tobio shouted, "Everyone on Earth thinks it's you who should rule the Land of Wizards!"

The wizard sat back down. One of his tentacles was rolling and unrolling repeatedly around his leg. Tobio thought it was a sign of interest, but he was still surprised to hear the wizard ask him:

"Who are you?"

"I am a child of Earth and…"

Down below, on the path, Sirius and the fay were running away.

"… and I'm so glad, so glad… to have seen you! Goodbye, Great Wizard, I'm going back home to talk about you."

"Not so fast, microbe. First, you'll eat with me, then I'll show you my domain."

"But, Great Wizard, I feel so dirty. Can I go wash up in the river that runs through your garden?"

"My word, you talk as stupidly as a sorcerer. What is all this about washing up before eating? Be careful not to annoy me with these stupidities. Let's go eat."

Truko dragged his visitor into a square tower, sat him down on a chair of nettles and spoke to him like he was sharing a secret.

"Just wait, I'm going to offer you a little pick-me-up drink. You're sure to like it."

"Oh, Great Wizard, I'm a little young to have alcohol."

"Moronic microbe, who said anything about alcohol! I'm talking about a bit of young blood. Fay blood, very fresh, you'll see."

Terrifying noises filled the castle after the wizard left. Soon he was back howling and waving his limbs. His skin was purple, his bristly hair standing on end, which he was plucking out furiously, his nose was flaring and his eyes blazing.

"Look, down there, that way, I saw a lady running away," said Tobio, purposefully misdirecting the Wizard.

Truko ran out in the same direction, followed by a swarm of squealing eagles. But he didn't forget to lock the tower when he left. Tobio was a prisoner. No worries. Wasn't he an expert scout? He tried to forget about fear, ridiculous fear that snuffed out courage and wore down intelligence. He took out his flashlight and sent a message to his mentor.

"Get ready, I'm coming."

Then he opened the window and tossed out his ball of thick string into the garden, holding onto one end, which he tied tightly with a scout's knot to an iron hook. Like a little monkey he shimmied down to the ground and in no time was in the bushes hiding the sectaphore. Hands shook each other firmly, eyes looked at each other proudly and tenderly.

The machine took off at record speed and Tobio, surprised and shy, stared at the extraordinary little fay sleeping soundly in the back.

A prick in this thigh made him yelp.

"Good grapes, mentor, did you forget the souvenir you promised Spruce?"

Sirius looked crestfallen but lightened up when he saw Tobio proudly pull a bunch of bristles out of his pants pocket.

CHAPTER IV
At home with the sorcerer Sirius

They gave Tobio an enthusiastic welcome at the King of the Fays' castle when Sirius told how he had acted during the expedition. Spruce and Zalou became his fast friends.

"But it's time I went back to my country," the sorcerer said. "You're still coming with me, aren't you, Tobio?"

"I've been looking forward to seeing your country, mentor.

"So let's go! We'll get there in time for the welcome."

Tobio carried a bag full of gifts. Spruce had made a lovely outfit, short pants woven from green fibers and a soft shirt made of cream silk. Zalou had given him a pair of magic sandals and the King a black stone that emitted soft, warm, dark red rays for an hour every day—it was a precious talisman that made the bearer invulnerable to all kinds of wizard spells.

The sectaphore started off slowly while the smiling fays sprinkled the travelers with flowers as a way of saying goodbye. They climbed a hill, then down the other side and Tobio, to his great surprise, was among the beasts he'd first seen on his arrival on Jupiter.

"We'll have to fly over the Land of the Beasts," Sirius said, "otherwise we'll never get through the crowds of curious creatures who want to get a look at you."

Tobio admired the beautiful calves with wet snouts and innocent eyes who were pestering their moms and romping around.

The animals are really happy here, he thought.

Sirius landed on a high plain that stretched out very far in the distance. It was slashed with deep, wild canyons. In one of them they could see a weird castle built on a steep rock.

"That's the domain of the sprite Torrent, Tobio."

"What's he like?"

The sorcerer answered laughing, "Look, there he is now."

Indeed, a kind of giant with a long, gray beard and flowing hair was coming forward, waving his arms. Sirius stopped the sectaphore and got out to greet the sprite whose voice was booming:

"Hello, neighbor, good to see you again. I can't sit still this morning. I have to keep moving."

"You're right, Torrent, you…"

But the sprite was already gone, stomping away in a hurry.

"That dear old neighbor," Sirius said, "is always worked up but he has a heart of gold. But we're here now. Let's leave the sectaphore and walk."

A row of proud pine trees guarded the entrance to the sorcerer's domain. At the sight of their master, they filled the air with fragrance and the warblers, chaffinches and chickadees came from every direction, gathered together and launched into the welcome hymn. On the high branches, the squirrels beat time with their tails. Tiny strawberries, hiding in the foliage, turned bright red. The moss became soft and purred while the mushrooms, who wanted to celebrate too, made holes in it by thumping their heads.

"Oh, mentor, everything around your home is so wonderful to see and hear and smell!"

The two friends went down a wide path plushly covered in pine needles. At the end, on a small hill from which they could see the whole area, was the sorcerer's house. It was a simple building, wide, low, with a huge roof and a tall chimney that was exhaling pleasant smoke.

"This, mentor, is a real house!"

A short, round, pink and smiling man came out to meet them.

"This is my friend Mocco, Tobio. You can't help but love him. He's always in a good mood and good-natured. Mocco, this is my ward, Tobio, a strong boy with guts and a lot of common sense."

Tobio held out his hand to the man who was very likable with his double chin and dimples. And the feeling must have been mutual because Mocco promised to show Tobio a lot of interesting things after the welcome.

Then there were Kapi and Kapette, Sirius' two big, brown dogs who bounded up, wild with joy. Aster, his favorite mare, smelled his beloved master from the field where he was grazing and came galloping up to him, snorting and whinnying. A few curious gazelles poked their heads out from a clump of trees. And then a black animal came out of nowhere and hurled itself into Tobio's legs, knocking him over.

"Oh, the little devil, where did it go?"

Sirius laughed his head off and grabbed the wriggling billy goat.

"This is Mephisto, the naughty one, the jealous one. Except that he's a good kind. He saved me once from a goat bewitched by the terrible sprite Gribus and since then, we've been friends. Come on now, make your peace."

Tobio felt a deep dislike for the ugly beast with mean and shifty eyes, but to please his mentor he gave in and petted his head. Ugh, what an awful feeling! A jolt of disgust ran through his arm.

Friendly Mocco noticed this and sent Mephisto and the three others into the house where a most delicious meal was waiting for them in a comfortable room. Kapette rubbed his head against Tobio's leg and stayed by his side so that from then on the sorcerer could take care of Kapi. Tobio's heart leapt with joy because he had dreamed for so long of having a dog friend.

"It's agreed, Tobio, I'm giving you Kapette," Sirius had guessed what he was thinking.

"That's the best present ever! Thank you so much, mentor! And thanks too for the wonderful welcome. My compliments!"

"It's Mocco you should thank. He loves eating. Oh, don't blush, Mocco. I wouldn't have it any other way because the more you eat, the more cheerful and kind you become. Keep it up. But I'm sorry I'll have to leave you. I've been gone for a month and I've got a lot of things to do. Mocco, be kind enough to show Tobio my domain, then set him up in the green pavilion."

"As you wish and see you later, Sirius. Call us if you need any help."

Like two old comrades, Tobio and Mocco walked away laughing.

"First, I'll show you my place, Earth boy, and you tell me if you like it."

"Let's go, Jupiter man."

"Look, there's my private path. I'll bet you've never seen another like it."

A path made of nails, side by side, points up, running through thick bushes.

"I have no desire to walk on that. The soles of my shoes are very thin."

"Be quiet, skeptical Earth boy. Take my hand and follow me."

Tobio was amazed to be able to walk on the carpet of nails like on ice.

Because he was astonished, Mocco whispered to him, "Hey, did you think I was a sorcerer for nothing!"

A little house, as clear as crystal showed up. They could see a beautiful red sitting room inside and Mocco sitting in an armchair reading a book.

"Hold on, is that your twin?" Tobio asked.

"Maybe. Let's go say hello anyway."

Mocco gave three soft raps on the door and it opened. Filled with wonder, Tobio entered a room carpeted with moss from which grew bunches of violets and primroses. In one corner were two nightingales practicing a new serenade they were going to dedicate to the stars. Four dwarves sprang out of a flowering bush to offer them a refreshing beverage in flowers called Lady's mantle.

"Am I dreaming, Mocco? Where's the red sitting room?"

"That was another spell, Tobio. And since we're here, where no one can hear us, I'll tell you a secret. It was after that nasty goat stayed there that I came to live here. He was there for only two days when Sirius had to go to the Land of the Fays. So, I stayed there alone with the dwarves who take care of the domain. Can you believe it? It was impossible for me to go anywhere without that beast on my heels, spying on me day and night."

"It's strange, Mocco. I, too, don't like Mephisto. I have the feeling he's mean and shifty. We'll have to warn my mentor right away. Come on, let's put off the visit until tomorrow."

"I think you're right, Tobio, let's go. We'll pass by the green pavilion where you can clean up a bit since the dwarves have already put your bags there."

"Oh, Mocco, do I have dwarves too?"

"Of course, Tobio, six of them and all very jolly."

"The little dears, I like them already."

Tobio couldn't hold back a cry of joy when he finally saw the pavilion. It looked like a big cabin made of leaves with lots of round windows. But it was solidly built. On the roof was a cuckoo squawking. In front of the door, in a little pond, ducks were splashing around. There were even tiny ones going fast and as light as flakes of wool. Silky, playful kittens frolicked on the lawn, playing hide-and-go-seek with every insect they saw.

Tobio was delighted. He asked, "Are they mine too?"

"Of course, just like Kapette who's running around over there. Say, what's got into her?"

The good dog came up to Tobio, lay down at his feet and howled. Then she got up and tugged his arm, all the while still howling.

"Mocco, let's go! Let's run! I hope nothing's happened to my mentor!"

In the house there was no sign of Sirius but the muddy footprints of a goat led Tobio and Mocco into the sorcerer's workroom. It was a mess. The table and chairs were overturned. Mocco looked for something in a small cabinet. He turned around, his face beaming.

"Nothing to fear, Tobio, our friend isn't in danger but there'll be trouble for whoever transformed into a goat to attack him."

"What are you talking about?"

"Well, look, Sirius managed to find a way to duplicate himself. He tried it in front of me and it was perfect. He swallowed a black pill and a few seconds later his form or, if you prefer, his body lay motionless on the ground. He himself was invisible, watching me. The pills were kept in a box that looked like an ordinary rock. So, the rock isn't in its place. Get it?"

"But Mocco, what if the goat took it?"

"Impossible, Tobio. It's got a spell on it, meaning that to take it you have to do it in a special way that even I don't know."

"Is that Kapi barking happily?"

Tobio ran and threw himself into the arms of his mentor. Since he was sniffling, Sirius told him, "There, there, my boy, everything's fine."

"It's just that I was almost afraid."

Mocco came up panting and the sorcerer asked them to follow him to the statue of Gribus. At the far end of the domain, he stopped in front of a big, black, ugly stone and said to them:

"Gribus, the traitor, will have to stay like this for ten years as punishment for his viciousness and for abusing my kindness and hospitality."

CHAPTER V
The Lord of Beasts is happy

It had already been a month since Tobio had become a guest of his mentor, Sirius. Time seemed to fly by, what with his two friends, the dwarves and the animals. Today he was very excited because he had just found in the library a book written by an old magician that talked about a question that fascinated him. The author claimed that it existed somewhere in the mountains a red pearl belonging to the Lord of Beasts that allowed its owner to hear what animals were thinking and to understand their language.

In the morning, after the dew, Tobio told this to his mentor and said, "Mentor, I'd really like to have this pearl. How should I get it?"

"My boy, it's not dangerous, but it'll take kindness and intelligence. I'll let you deal with it alone. Go find the chief of my dwarves, Zimboom, he'll be able to tell you which mountain it is. Then get ready and prove yourself worthy of my teachings."

"Thanks, mentor, goodbye and you won't be disappointed."

Zimboom lived in a house built of pine branches. When Tobio arrived, the dwarf was standing in front of his door, smoking a pipe, his nose and cheeks puffing out, a lock of hair sticking out of his cap and straight into the air.

"Hello, Zozio," he said because he couldn't pronounce "t", "p", "b" and "d".

"Hello, chief, I need some information. My mentor told me you knew all about the mountains."

"Of course he did, Zozio. Did you know that one of my ancestors was the King of Dwarves? He was called Ziriri and had 28 sons and 15 daughters. His first son was Fuxy, married to Princess Zaza, the second…"

"That's very interesting, Zimboom. You can tell me everything in detail later. Right now, I'd like to know where the mountain is that's the home of the Lord of Beasts."

"It's not far from here, Zozio. You take the path that goes through the forest, then you'll see three mountains. It's the middle one you have to climb."

"Thanks a lot, chief, and if you ever need anything, think of me."

Now Tobio was in front of said mountain. He marched up the blue slopes but was surprised to find that he wasn't going anywhere. He was literally walking in place. After an hour of useless effort he sat down, crestfallen.

"Oh la la, he's a clumsy one! That really hurt!"

Tobio jumped to his feet, startled, looking all around for the source of the voice. He saw nothing but a big green beetle rubbing its claws vigorously. He thought to himself, *What a pretty bug, did I hurt it?*

Then he picked it up gingerly and examined it.

"Look at my leg, meany! You crushed it!"

"Oh, I'm sorry, beetle," Tobio was confused. "I'm so sorry. What can I do fix it?"

"You do plenty just by saying you're sorry for what you did… unintentionally, I'm sure. Why are you here?"

"I was trying to climb this mountain to get the red pearl."

"Well, drop to the ground and climb on my back."

And the beetle puffed up, puffed up so much and so big that Tobio could climb onto him like a horse.

Halfway up the mountain the bug stopped and said, "I can't go any farther, my friend, because I can't go into the realm of rocks."

"I'm very thankful for what you've done for me, kind beetle. I'll try to get the rest of the way on my own."

The beetle disappeared and Tobio went on. Now there was nothing but steep rocks and raging rivers everywhere. It was impossible to pass between them. Suddenly he saw a trout who had missed a jump and was washed up on flat rock, still fidgeting and breathing. Taking pity on him Tobio put him back in the water.

"You're a good person, boy," said the fish. "Get on my back and I'll take you to the top."

The trout puffed up, puffed up so much and so big that Tobio could sit on him. Grabbing onto his fins, he reached the top in ten jumps. There was no time to thank the helpful fish because he swam off right away.

Tobio stood in front of a pile of pearls of all colors. As he was picking one up, a beautiful red one, a tall old man with blue eyes and rosy cheeks showed up.

He asked quietly, "What are you doing, child?"

"Excuse me. I didn't see anyone around and thought I could take one of these pearls. There are so many of them."

"It'll be of no use to you, child, except to please your eyes. I guard the real pearl."

"Oh, please give it to me."

"I'd like to because you're a good person but on one condition—that you spend a few days on Earth with it. Your mentor will show you how. One week will be enough. Then the pearl will be yours."

"Very well, I'll do what you ask."

Then the Sprite held out a tiny crystal ball in which the magic pearl was twinkling like a star.

"I'm so happy!" exclaimed Tobio.

But he was alone. At his feet he saw a narrow path that he took to reach the foot of the mountain. He got to his mentor's when he was sitting down for the welcome.

"Already back, Tobio? And from the look on your face you've got your coveted treasure."

"I do, mentor, but it'll only be mine after I've spent a week with you on Earth."

"What great timing! I was going to invite your family here."

"Dear mentor!" Tobio was almost crying with joy. "How did you know that I missed them?"

"I just had to hear all your sighs lately."

"Can we leave today?"

"Certainly."

"How will we get there?"

"The King of the Fays' magic chariot. It'll get us there in less than an hour. I'll let theKking know so he can send it to me. Go and get ready."

Tobio put his scout's clothes back on. He was barely ready when the dwarves came running up to him.

"The magic chariot is here!"

"Let's go and I'll set you up."

Tobio saw nothing but a big, shimmering ball like a giant soap bubble.

"Sit here, Tobio, close your eyes and say aloud where you want to go."

"Mentor, I'd like to go back to the garden near the pine tree from where I left."

And Tobio, utterly amazed once again, was there. Just like when he left, the geraniums were in bloom and the roses filling the air with their perfume.

A gentle voice came out of the pine tree, "Stay calm, my dears, the boy is back. Don't let him know you're here or else he'll stay by our nest to look at you and touch you. I'm so scared that I'm losing the will to live."

Tobio knew that the blackbird and her chicks were up there on the third branch. He didn't want to cause the bird any more trouble, so without looking up he left.

It was so nice to see mama, papa, brother and sister again and to give them big hugs. Thankfully they hadn't been worried because a good fay had told them what had happened to Tobio, who told them they would stay together from now on because his mentor had invited everyone to come visit his domain in one week.

"Bravo! Hurrah!" the whole family shouted together.

Exhausted now, Tobio went to sleep. When he woke up in the morning, he was surprised to hear a high voice saying, "Goodbye, dear friend, and thanks a lot for the fine meal, as fresh and sweet as could be."

"Goodbye and come back tonight, we'll go at the other side."

At the same time that he felt a sharp sting on his cheek, Tobio saw two nasty mosquitoes flying away. Furious, he went after them with a pillow and fought until they both lay dying.

"Stay calm, sisters," said a big fly perched on the lamp, "the boy's feeling aggressive today. We might meet the same fate as our stupid, greedy cousins. But what's he going to say when he sees that the bratty old moth laid her eggs in his pretty ski outfit?"

"Good grapes!" Tobio yelled as he opened his cabinet. "What've we got here?"

Disaster! The pants he was so proud of, that fit him so well, looked like a sieve!

"Wretched vermin! Cursed riffraff!"

Tobio crushed the plump, gorged larvae.

From one corner the mother groaned, "Oh, humans! Why won't they understand that we were created to make them neat and generous. All the neglected clothes, all the old things they accumulate out of greed, belong to us."

After cleaning up Tobio went into the garden. On the table, next to the creamy chocolate, was a letter that said that the whole family had already left for the sorcerer's castle, and he had to stay alone on Earth during the week. He was sorry he wouldn't be there to see their joy when they got to the wonderful land.

To shake off his melancholy, he decided to take a stroll through the fields. On the way, his attention was caught by a toad having a hard time moving.

The creature looked up at him with pretty golden eyes and said, "Are you going to hurt me too? Have pity! Look, I'm wounded, sick and so unhappy. I cried and suffered all night long after a kid came yesterday and hit my soft skin with a stick just for fun."

Tobio leaned over, picked him up tenderly and placed him under a big, protective leaf. As he stood back up he heard a whine and saw a cricket trying to limp around a clump of grass.

"Only one leg, what's going to happen to me? No more crazy jumping in the sweet-smelling meadows, no more life because I'll soon fall prey to my worst enemies since I can't get away from them anymore."

And then a sad groan came from a dying butterfly—his wings were wrinkled, ruined. He had been used for a second as a toy by a selfish brat who didn't understand that every time he saw this living flower, this miracle of nature, in its graceful flight, he should've given a prayer of thanks to the creator instead of destroying the creature and acting like a brute.

Tobio knew now why the Lord of Beasts had demanded that he spend a week on Earth. It was no fun. He wanted to run away from the field bathed in radiant sunlight where the flowers scented the air and the children sowed suffering.

But Tobio's heart was knocking hard at the door of his conscience and endlessly repeating, "Running away in the face of suffering is cowardly. You have to fight to relieve the suffering, to abolish it. Keep walking the roads and the fields, lean down over the poor wounded creatures of flesh and blood, listen to their pleas, their cries. Take a pencil and piece of paper and write to all the children of Earth what you've seen and heard. Their little hearts are still good and gentle. They'll understand and instead of being torturers of animals, they'll become their friends and protectors."

Tobio thought, *That's exactly what I'll do*.

"Bravo," whispered the voice of the Sprite in his ear.

CHAPTER VI
Tobio, King of the Gribouillons

When he got back to the house Tobio heard a magpie crying out to his friend from the top of a branch of a pine tree.

"Come here and look at this incredible thing. What colors! Too bad it's so big, I'd like to decorate my nest with it."

Tobio walked over, full of curiosity. What good fortune! The chariot of the King of the Fays was back, waiting for him. Without a second thought he jumped in and shouted, "As fast as possible to Jupiter!"

The big ball vanished before the stupefied eyes of the magpie who was speechless with his beak dropped open.

A jolt! Tobio was sitting in a clearing. He wondered where in his mentor's domain he could be. To orient himself he first followed a path that went through a thick forest. Suddenly he saw a little house, as red as a strawberry, in the shade of a conifer. As he got closer a funny little woman, no taller than a dwarf, with a pointy bun of red hair on her head, eyes like blueberries and dressed in ruby-red clothes, came out and spoke in a high-pitched voice:

"Thank you, Great Sirius, for sending me a helper so quickly. Come in and quench your thirst, it's so hot! I forgot to tell you that I'm the fay Pygmenile. My father, the sprite Pyrhus, nicknamed Purple because he loves the color red so much, just left for the Land of Eternal Rest. He was the protector of the Gribouillons. I wanted to take his place and so came to live here. But after only one week, I left. They've all got such nasty flaws that it's impossible for a normal woman to live with them. When I talked with the sorcerer Sirius, who's always got good advice, he told me: 'Stay calm and if you want I'll send a king who will know how to knock some sense into them. So, go back now.'"

Tobio, who couldn't believe it, followed the fay into a room lined with geographic maps of unknown lands. On the ground, huge purple cushions took the place of chairs. On a table sat a glass three-quarters full of a greenish liquid, waiting. The fay offered it to him and after only two swallows, Tobio fell asleep…

He woke up bright and early, stretched and thought, "Oh, how soft it is."

He opened his eyes, squinted, and punched the pillow to clear his vision. Then he sat up and remembered. He was king! What would his school chums say if they could see him in this red satin bed, sitting on a platform that looked out on a huge room? Tobio started laughing.

"Hey, is anybody in this palace?"

Three men wearing purple pants and wrinkled green jackets came running, pushing a cart on which was the king's breakfast. Tobio looked at the dishes. They might have been quite pretty but at the moment they were chipped and dirty.

Looking at the oldest of the Gribouillons who was staring at him with his little, round, dark eyes and muttering behind his curly red beard, Tobio asked, "What's your name?"

"Ogro, Majesty."

"Well, Ogro, I have to tell you that I never eat in bed unless I'm sick. Go and set the table for me. But keep in mind, the table has to be clean, the dishes too, and unbroken, and everything has to be served properly. I hate things to be dirty and I'll definitely get angry if you don't do exactly as I say."

Waving over the two others, who had thin, scrunched up faces, the king said:

"You, bring me my clothes after brushing them. What's your name?"

"Menil, Sire."

To the last one who looked more awake and was called Ratouille, Tobio asked for water to wash himself.

"But Majesty, we can't get any water except from the river and it's cold this early."

"That's what I need," the king replied. "Nothing better to wake me up and put me in a good mood. Take a few men with you and get me a good bucket."

"Oh, Majesty, it's just that everyone's still sleeping."

"When the sun is shining and the birds singing? What lazy bones! Is there an alarm bell in this land?"

"Three, Sire."

"Start ringing them. How many people are living here?"

"40,000, Sire."

"Make sure everyone is here in an hour. I'm going to talk to them."

"Very well, Sire."

"Another thing, Ratouille, tell Ogro and Menil that if they're not properly dressed and cleaned up tomorrow morning, I'll give them a good thrashing. The same goes for you. Got it?"

"Yes, Sire."

Despite the inferior cleanliness of everything, the new king had to admit that the food was excellent. Sitting up very straight in his silk outfit, he took his role seriously.

He said, "First of all, I have to set an example, then demand that they follow it. Laziness will be abolished from my realm otherwise we'll never get anywhere."

The bells were ringing outside the open windows. Someone in the street was shouting, "The new king is here! He wants to talk to everyone! Get up! Get up!"

Tobio finished his breakfast. The big room was still empty. When he looked out the windows he saw that the grass and the leaves of the trees were red. It wasn't so surprising. He was starting to get used to this color. But now the door swung open and a Gribouillon came in.

"Well," Tobio said, "you're the first. I've been waiting for an hour. What's your name?"

"Bixy, Majesty."

"OK, Bixy, you'll be my Prime Minister. Find a big book to write down the names, in alphabetical order, of all the people of the land. You'll leave the book here and every morning you'll have to the first one here for the roll call."

Bixy had no time to answer before another arrived, followed by a third and fourth Gribouillon.

"Come here," the king told them, "and tell me your names."

"Torras."

"Cracus."

"Okkas."

"Torras, you look strong and brave. You'll be my chief of police. You can get a notebook and every morning write the names of anyone who misses roll call. Unless they have an emergency, they'll have to stand out in the town square for an hour in their nightshirts. I'll choose ten police officers to help you carry out my sentences. If you decide to make your men work instead of you, you'll go without food for ten days. Whoever won't work, won't eat.

"You, Cracus and Okkas, you'll deal with the women. Every household must be kept neat and clean. Along with big fines, the lazy will be forced to wear yellow dresses printed with the following words: Laziness is the mother of all vices! I'll visit every family personally once a year, unannounced. Make sure my orders are carried out fairly but strictly."

Since the room was full now, the king introduced his ministers, named the men who would help them and gave a short speech.

"Here I am at the request of Pygmenile, as your protector, your king. I come from Earth and I am also familiar with the Land of the Fays and the lands of sorcerers, wizards and dwarves. Everywhere I've been I've seen order, cleanliness and activity which brings prosperity, happiness and progress. What's more beautiful than a clean, neat woman, a tidy house and children with healthy hair, white teeth and freshly scrubbed hands? What's more calming than a pretty, flowery garden and a town with fresh air and well swept streets? What's more satisfying than well-ordered affairs? What's more appetizing than a well-served meal? What's more noble than a gentleman? You all know that a real gentleman is as decent and wholesome on the inside as much as on the outside. I want my people to be good, honest men and women and healthy, happy children. For this I've already made a few laws that my ministers will tell you about. I hope you accept them with good cheer because they're for the benefit and happiness of everyone. Every Thursday afternoon I'll be here to listen gladly to any one of my subjects who has a complaint or a request. Justice and wisdom will do everything possible to satisfy them. So be it!"

"Long live the king! Long live the king!" the Gribouillons shouted.

Blushing, Tobio bowed deeply.

One month had passed since the coming of the new king. In the beginning the town square was packed in the morning with men in their nightshirts. On the other hand, no punished women were seen in the streets but rather behind closed doors as more than one husband sneered gleefully at the yellow figure of his companion.

Everything soon got back to normal and the king became the idol of the Gribouillons. Laziness had been banished from the kingdom, all men were working, all women too since the ones without children helped the ones with many. Since there were no more parasites and everyone did the job he or she was physically and mentally capable of, everything that needed to get done, got done and benefited everyone.

Tobio had nothing more to do but watch the wheels spinning on their own and never stopping. Now he was thinking seriously about returning to his mentor and his family. But why wasn't the fay showing up? How could he contact her?

All of a sudden, the door swung open and Pygmenile stood before him, all smiles.

"I'm so glad to see you again, good fay. You can take my place now that everything's in order."

"Not exactly, Majesty. Like the true Earth child you are, you forgot about school. You haven't visited the school even once."

"That's because I had enough of it on Earth."

Pygmenile kept smiling and replied, "Do me the pleasure of visiting a school today. I'll come back tonight and you can tell me what you found."

Without wasting another second, Tobio left the palace and headed for the nearest school. He got there at the moment the students were going out for recess. How good he felt to see them playing and shouting! He remembered the fun times playing dodge ball, leapfrog and all the other games with his friends. He suddenly wanted to run and jump and play but was that really fitting for a king?

He thought, *This is the last time they'll get me to be king.*

Then, nearby, he saw a small, pale, poorly dressed boy looking enviously at the big, juicy piece of fruit his chum was eating.

"Good grapes!" Tobio cried out, "I've found what's wrong here."

The voice of the king echoed through the tumult and the games stopped; the children ran over.

"Go tell your teachers to meet me in the conference room. I want to talk to them. Then you can leave. I'm giving you the day off. As for you, little boy, what's your name?"

"Mounet."

"What's your father do?"

The boy answered proudly, "He writes stories about animals. My papa's very smart."

"Have you got any brothers or sisters?"

"Yes, indeed, ten of them."

"Hurry and go fetch your father and tell him to meet us in the conference room."

Arrhus, the father of Mounet, arrived out of breath and as pale as his little boy. The teachers with their airs of intelligence waited impatiently for what the king had to say.

Tobio stood up. All eyes were riveted on him. It was the most glorious time of his life—he was about to tell teachers what to do! When his eyes fell upon Arrhus, his pride vanished.

"Teachers," he said, "I want to introduce you to my Minister of Education, the writer Arrhus, who will see to it that you respect the new school rules. As follows:

"1: All children, no exceptions, will wear the same uniform depending on their age. I'll send you drawings.

"2: For all families with more than three children, these uniforms will be free, except for families who are rich.

"3: At 10 a.m. and 4 p.m. every child will be served a glass of milk, a piece of bread and some fruit. It's forbidden for children to bring anything from home.

"4: The top ten students of every class will be accepted into the higher schools at the expense of the State.

"5: Bad students will have to appear before the king.

"6: There will be a special tax on wealthy families without children to help the poorer ones."

All the teachers accepted these measures enthusiastically.

That evening, while Tobio was going back to the palace with his new minister, he was surprised to hear laughter coming from the brightly lit sitting room.

His mentor, who was waiting for him at the front gate, told him, "Tobio, my ward, my friend, I'm so proud of you! I wanted to be the first to shake your hand!"

"Oh, mentor, we'll stay together from now on, won't we?"

"As long as possible, my boy. But come, the King of the Fays, Spruce, Zalou and Mocco came to congratulate you. The fay Pygmenile is giving a big feast in your honor at the palace tonight."

When he walked in Tobio was applauded, congratulated and complimented. The King named him the secret detective of the Land of the Fays, a position for him and his mentor alone. He blushed with joy. What exciting adventures lay in store!

Pygmenile, in the name of all her people, gave him back the royal crown fashioned with a single ruby and said, "I will watch over the Gribouillons in the future but you will forever remain their Great King!"

In a corner of the room Arrhus shyly wiped away a tear.

CHAPTER VII
The magic wand that disappeared

Tobio had been back at his mentor's home for two days now with his family. Pierrot, the youngest, made friends with the dwarves. They were so much friendlier than the children on Earth; they never fought with each other or said nasty things. His big sister, Josette, spent a lot of time with Spruce, her mentor, who spoiled her greatly. His papa became a friend to the birds and had long conversations with Mocco. His mama was so amazed by all the beauty that she started writing about it in a big book.

Tobio, for today, had planned to visit the oldest sorcerer, Rochepic, but a messenger from the King of the Fays arrived asking him and his mentor to go to the palace at once. They didn't discuss the King's orders. In no time, the two secret detectives were with him.

The King was worried and in a bad mood. "My friends, look, is this my magic wand?"

Sirius and Tobio examined the object and declared that it was, indeed, the King's wand.

"My thief is therefore very clever because what you see here is a perfect fake. See, my wand performs miracles and has a current of love and harmony, whereas this one feels like it was made by the Devil's hands. This morning, when I wanted to use it to heal my horse, who was having eye problems, it transformed into an angry snake. I ended up putting it in a crystal box and the whole thing turned black."

"But your wand couldn't have been stolen last night, Majesty, because when you sleep, it is charged with a current so strong that nobody could hold it without becoming paralyzed."

"I thought so too, Sirius, and I believe the substitution must've happened yesterday. But when? I didn't leave the palace all day!"

"If I recall, Majesty, yesterday was your day of audience. Who came to see you?"

"The fays Josuette, Zikette and Brisette were the first. We had a nice chat. In the afternoon, the sorcerer Oleas came to submit a new spell, then the little gray wizard along with a ridiculously long creature offered me the respects of the Wizard King and a present. The sprite Phenox, who is the handsomest man on the planet, asked me for my approval to marry the fay Sisi. I gave it to them and we spent the evening celebrating the event."

"Excuse me, Majesty, I have to tell Tobio that the gray wizard lives in the palace of Ramines X, the Wizard King, and that he acts as his advisor."

"But then it's so simple," Tobio cried out. "The extraordinary creature that came with the wizard must have caught the attention of our king while the wizard did his nasty deed."

"That's very possible, Tobio," said the King, "because I was enraptured by the creature."

"The best thing to do," Sirius said, "would be to send me to the Wizard King for some reason, Majesty. That way, I could go there and do some digging."

"You're right, Sirius, take this ring and offer it to him on my behalf. Don't forget to thank him for his present and tell him I was very pleased."

"Very well, Majesty. See you soon."

The two friends were so happy to climb into the sectaphore! After a twelve-hour trip at record speed they reached the Land of Wizards. The castle of the Wizard

King was right in the middle, on a hill whose top was flat and the slopes steep and smooth like walls, therefore inaccessible.

The sectaphore landed gently in front of the main entrance to the palace and with all spikes out, full of fluid, it waited there for the two passengers to accomplish their mission.

Tobio had never seen a castle like this. It was square, made of polished, shiny metal with big, misshapen windows through which nothing could be seen from the outside. When they approached the door, it opened and soldiers dressed in iron came out and formed two lines.

Tobio shuddered. "Mentor, they've got no heads!"

Indeed, looking at the whole body and the helmet in the right place, the heads were not visible.

"Don't worry, my boy, let's go in."

Tobio gritted his teeth and boldly followed his mentor down a big, dark hallway. He was constantly being brushed by something cold and sticky so he was relieved when they finally reached the throne room.

It was perfectly square, apparently made of platinum just like the throne on which a gigantic eagle perched. On the ground some big, black crocodiles were wrestling. But what Tobio was watching was the King. He was very tall, breathtakingly beautiful with black hair, totally white skin and perfectly harmonious features. His black silk clothes, his heavy, dark cape and the huge, pitch-black jewel he wore on his left ring finger made him look sinister and spectacular.

"When I was on Earth, this is how I pictured the Devil," Tobio said as he followed his mentor to the foot of the throne of Ramines X. The King, who had so far made no movement, stood up and his deeply ironic laughter echoed eerily through the room.

"Look here," he said, "to what do I owe the honor of your visit, great Sirius?"

The sorcerer answered calmly, smiling, "Greetings from the King of the Fays, Your Majesty. He would like to present you with this ring that you once admired so much."

"That is very kind. Thank him profusely for me and please sit down."

"Not before informing you of my whole mission, Majesty. My king also asks that you give back his magic wand that was obviously taken away by mistake by the Gray Wizard."

"As you wish, Sirius. Come and see: it's in the exhibition room where all my subjects got to admire it last night because I gave a big feast in its honor. We had a lot of laughs, I assure you."

"Quite likely, Majesty. The wand has the power to make the people around it happy and cheerful."

In the middle of the room full of glass cabinets containing the rarest and most precious objects, the King of the Fays' magic wand was stuck into a big cauliflower covered with magnificent blossoms.

At this sight Ramines X furrowed his brow and sneezed.

"The flowers probably bother you, Majesty," said Sirius. "What do you expect! The wand is used to beauty and where there isn't any, it creates some."

Tobio had stopped in front of a flashy little stand on which sat a mesmerizing green eye, which drew him closer. As Sirius and the King were busy together, he snatched it and dropped it in his pocket.

"Phooey!" Ramines X said. "Take this perverted wand back to its owner, Sirius."

"Very well, Majesty. Congratulations."

Without looking back Tobio and his mentor hurried back to the sectaphore. During the trip back the sorcerer was surprised that Tobio was so quiet and asked him why.

"It's because of the eye, mentor."

"What eye?"

"The one that was gaudily displayed!"

"I see. It was probably the famous talisman of Ramines X. Why is it bothering you so much?"

"Because I have it in my pocket, mentor."

Sirius opened his mouth but no sound came out. He slapped his thighs hard, a habit he had to regain his composure, and cried out, "Unbelievable! Wonderful! Tobio, you're one-of-a-kind! Ha, ha, ha! What do they say on Earth?"

"He laughs best who laughs last, mentor."

"That's it, my boy. And we're laughing, we're laughing…"

For a short while the sectaphore hadn't been working the way it should. Sirius was starting to worry because it was the first time it had happened.

"I've got an idea, mentor. We're right above the island of the sprite Oax. Since he's one of our friends, let's go down and say hello. You can look for the problem at the same time."

"You're right, Tobio, better safe than sorry."

The sprite had seen them coming and was waiting for them. He was right there to meet them by the time they landed.

"My dear Sirius, I'm so glad to see you again."

"Me too, Oax. This is Tobio, my ward; he's full of surprises. He comes from Earth."

"Welcome. Come inside."

Tobio had to control himself not to break down laughing at the sprite. He was so funny with his seal-like head, his tight clothes in scales like a fish and his chubby shape. Every sentence he spoke, he bowed as if to emphasize it, and he rubbed his hands. Since his feet were pretty big and webbed, he kept getting tripped up and stumbling headfirst before saving himself at the last moment.

When they got to the palace, Tobio gasped in admiration. A gigantic shell made of tons of opal, folded and spiraling in speechless harmony stood before him. The inside, colored aquamarine, was artistically decorated with coral and other pretty aquatic plants. In a splendid pool there were beautiful mermaids laughing and playing with a starfish.

"I do congratulate you. It's absolutely amazing here," Tobio said.

"It's the sea, my boy, nothing else like it."

"You can say that again."

"You had a good idea to come visit me, Sirius."

"I'm sorry to have to say that there was an ulterior motive. My machine is acting up and I had to stop."

"OK, we'll take a look at it soon. First, come have some welcome."

At the deliciously set table served by adorable mermaids, the visitors told Oax about their expedition. There was no reason to be discreet—all sorcerers were bound to spread the news with a hearty laugh.

"It deserves revenge," the sprite said, "otherwise it'll damage the prestige of our king."

"No need to worry, Oax, the King of the Fays will emerge as the winner. Tell all the sprites to come for the nectar tonight; all the sorcerers and fays will be there too."

When Sirius examined his sectaphore, he was surprised to find nothing out-of-the-ordinary. When he turned it on, it was working normally. It was only when Tobio climbed into his seat that the engine started coughing again.

"I get it," the sorcerer exclaimed. "It's that lousy eye that's causing the problem. It is as toxic as its master. It's interfering with the device that captures solar energy. Go in the back and put it in the pastry box."

No sooner was the object shut away than the machine sped up and flew smoothly.

The King of the Fays and all the court were waiting on pins and needles for their return. When the long shape of the sectaphore appeared on the horizon, shouts of joy rang through the palace gardens.

Bowing deeply and very calmly, Sirius presented the King with his precious wand, then with Tobio, who was beaming and kept his hand in his pocket, he asked for a private meeting with the sovereign.

That night, the guests poured into the brightly lit palace. The door of the festival room was open for the people to come in. Soon, laughter was erupting everywhere.

But who was in charge of the table? No pretty flowers or rare perfumes. Only four rows of carrots, points up, guarding a nasty green eye. At one end of the table, facing the King, a seat remained vacant, but soon Ramines X came.

The King of the Fays greeted him kindly, "Thank you for accepting my invitation, Majesty. In fact, it's in your honor that I'm offering the nectar tonight. As a souvenir you can take my table decoration, it'll fit right into your gallery."

Everyone knew and looked at the Wizard King who was seething with rage. He went away muttering curses and threats.

The King of the Fays called after him, "Come on, Ramines, be a good sport. There's always one who laughs first and one who laughs last. This time, happily for me, I got the last laugh."

The trail of the Wizard King's dark cape disappeared.

The puckish fays merrily grabbed the carrots and held them high, shouting, "Long live the King! Long live our King!"

Then it was time to put their pearly whites to good use.

CHAPTER VIII
The end of the mad sorcerer

"It's strange that the sorcerer Oleas isn't here," the King said. "He worries me with his obsession to always find new spells. Maybe you should go pay him a visit, Sirius?"

"As you wish, Majesty."

"Don't forget to bring Tobio with you, of course."

"My inseparable companion? What do you think, Majesty?"

"Go and report back to me as soon as possible."

"Very well."

The two detectives arrived at Oleas' at the time of the welcome. Everything seemed peaceful on his property.

"Look," Sirius observed, "everything's changed since my last visit here. The bushes are growing every which way and the gravel path is overgrown with weeds. It looks like the place has been abandoned. And the forest, Tobio! Look at the forest! Where did it come from? It wasn't there a month ago! Oh, here's our friend in the flesh. Hello, Oleas. How are you? We were passing by and figured we'd pay you a visit."

"Hmm," the sorcerer replied as Tobio examined him carefully.

He was tall and thin, with short, spiky hair, a grisly beard and small, round eyes that were dark and darting and always blinking.

"Hello sorcerer," Tobio said. "I'm glad to meet you. I know you're the most exceptional sorcerer and I love sorcery."

Oleas loosened up. Wasn't it always good to meet someone with the same tastes?

"I know you're very busy, Sirius, so go about your business and leave the boy with me."

"I was going to propose the very thing, Oleas. Thanks for watching him. I'll pick him up on my way back."

"Of course, of course, see you later."

Tobio noticed that the sorcerer looked relieved when his mentor left and when the sectaphore had finally disappeared he looked downright jubilant.

"Before sitting down for the welcome, take a look at this forest, my boy. What do you say?"

"It looks perfect."

"Well, I created it."

"Marvelous. How did you do it?"

"After days of experimentation I finally found a potion that can change animals into plants."

"That's mighty clever!"

"Just wait, I'll show you more. Come on, we'll eat afterwards."

Tobio followed the sorcerer through the thick, deserted forest. In the end they got to a very high, discreetly concealed fence. After walking along it for thirty feet or more, they suddenly stood in front of a huge iron door. Trembling with excitement, Oleas had trouble putting the long key into the lock. But he got the door open and Tobio had to hold back a cry.

There were the most extraordinary creatures he had ever seen wandering around in the garden. Tiny, deformed bodies, twisted limbs, huge heads with pasty faces and big, round, bulging eyes. No nose but a mouth or more precisely a snout that never stopped moving.

Legs apart, arms dangling, watching in ecstasy the sorcerer gloated, "My work! Men! I've created men! And with what? With common critters, with frogs!"

"Unbelievable," Tobio managed to utter.

"Thank you for understanding and admiring me. You'll see, I'll do even better, then I'll flood the planet with my creatures and all the other races will disappear. Right now, I have to give them a king. Can't use an animal for that, I'll need a human. I chose you."

"Better and better," Tobio said. "But if you don't mind, I'd like to have the welcome one more time just as I am."

"If you accept my offer, I'll be glad to."

"As future king, I'd also like you to show me the key to my future kingdom. It looked very ingenious."

"Here it is. It's different because of its unusual length. You see, I had to make very thick walls and a special lock to protect my creation. Everyone is jealous of me!"

"That's understandable. So, how does the lock work?"

With the key in place, Tobio prepared his scout's punch, mustered all his courage and wham! The mad sorcerer was thrown back behind the door with his monsters.

At first, Tobio thought only of running away, but then he thought of his mentor who was coming back to fetch him. He had to stay there until then. Moreover, despite his many amazing adventures, a twelve-year-old boy needed to eat. So, he headed back to the castle to find some food.

After going down a long, dark hallway, he reached a big room where there was a table with beautiful fruit starting to go bad in a cup. Tobio prevented the disaster by eating them all. Feeling better, he kept searching and found, in an old cupboard, a plate of cookies. He would have preferred a pie, but when push came to shove cookies did the trick.

That was when he heard heavy footsteps approaching. Before he had time to even move, the door opened and a man of iron stood there. Tobio wasn't afraid of giants or wizards or anything made of flesh and blood but a man of iron, that was something else!

He thought fast. A metal creature couldn't come from God, so it was not under His protection, whereas he, Tobio, had a guardian angel always watching over him."

He felt stronger and asked the metal man in front of him, "Who are you?"

The giant toy raised a hand and struck his chest, groaning long and loudly. Then he grabbed Tobio's jacket and dragged him over to a small black door. He pointed to the lock and started moaning. Tobio understood and tried in vain to open the door with all the keys he could find. Suddenly his mentor's laugh exploded behind him.

"Well, my boy, you're doing fine. I haven't been gone an hour and here you are, trying to break into a door with some walking suit of armor. So, what's Oleas doing?"

"Mentor, he's crazy, so I locked him up with the monsters he created."

"What are you saying? Come and show me."

At these words the metal man exhaled some heartrending groans. Stupefied, Sirius examined him, then pulled out an iron hook from his pocket and put it in the lock of the small door, which opened up in no time.

There was a cramped, white room. It was completely empty but a monstrous light hung from the ceiling. The metal man went straight to a big dial that he tried in vain to turn. Tobio went to help and a spooky light flooded the room. The iron hand pushed Tobio and his mentor back into the shadows and the metal man collapsed in the middle of the light. Frightening howls started coming from the mass. Thicker, stringy rays poured out of the light. Now the metal man was no longer crying out but melting slowly away. The iron disappeared and the light went out. Lying on the ground, motionless, was a young man.

Sirius hurriedly tried to resuscitate him with light taps on his chest. Finally, he opened his eyes.

"Thank you, my friends. I owe you my life."

Sirius smiled, "Tobio, let me introduce you to the sorcerer Amor. I've been looking for him for three years unsuccessfully. The fay Vivette is going to be very happy to see you again. Poor thing, she's turned all pale and never laughs anymore."

Amor blushed and got to his feet. "Sirius, I can't leave before freeing the other prisoners. There should be three more. Let's go help them."

"Right you are, Amor. Where are they?"

"I don't know. We'll have to look for them."

"The fastest way," Sirius proposed, "would be to split up. The first one to find anything will call out."

"Got it."

Amor went upstairs while Sirius started searching around the room with the light. Tobio wasn't sure, thought about it, then ran out of the house and ducked into the supernatural forest. He remembered that he'd seen three pines among the birch trees. He'd even been bothered by the fact that his favorite trees could be created with a spell. They were still there, withered-looking, the branches drooping with few needles. Tobio leaned against one trunk but pushed away at once. Was it his imagination going wild or did he really feel the tree shiver when he touched it.

70

He tried again and this time there was no doubt: the whole trunk started vibrating.

"Mentor! Mentor!"

"I'm here. What's wrong?"

"Touch that tree."

The sorcerer did so and got the same effect.

"No doubt, my boy, we've found them. It seems you've got a nose for it."

Amor was there now, too.

Sirius said, "You two, don't move and don't interfere, no matter what you see. I'm going to try an antidote to the spell that the Great Spirit taught me."

Frozen in place, Tobio and Amor watched with their fists clenched.

Sirius stretched out his arms and shouted three times, "Oéva, Oéva, Oéva!" Then he bowed and repeated a long incantation. When he stood back up, very straight and noble, he ordered, "Let the spell be broken!"

A big wind rushed through the forest, the pine trees fell, the others vanished and bright lightning illuminated the scene. Thousands of croaking, jumping frogs covered the ground. Sirius cleared them away from the three bodies on the ground.

"My word, it's the wizard Nimbex and the sorcerers Mineas and Solex. Come on, friends, wake up!"

Everyone was safe and sound.

But Amor was angry and shouted, "Let's take Oleas to be judged by the King."

"Come with me," Tobio held up his long key.

The fence was easy to find, but he asked his mentor to open the door and go in first—he had no desire to see those awful creatures.

Sirius and the others were appalled. They'd never seen anything like it. All the monster (nearly thirty in all) were huddled around something on the ground. Their snouts were slurping and sloshing like mad and grunting with pleasure. When they saw the men, they moved away and Tobio glimpsed the empty clothes of Oleas.

"Mentor, let's get out of here! They ate him!"

The door was slammed shut.

Sirius just shook his head, "Poor devil, he was certainly mad, otherwise he wouldn't have tried to be the equal of the Creator of all things. We should only be a reflection of Him, nothing more. Let's go and report to the King."

CHAPTER IX
Tobio receives a magic potion from the Supreme Being

"What's on your mind, Tobio? For days you've been daydreaming and preoccupied."

"I'm thinking of the Great Spirit, mentor. You're the only one who's seen it, apparently."

"Seen is not the right word. I felt it and heard it. To see it you need a potion that the Supreme Being has, but how can you get it? It's better not to talk about it."

"Mentor, I think that would be a wonderful adventure. Daring something nobody else has dared! Overcoming an incredible obstacle! Erasing the word IMPOSSIBLE! Oh, mentor, it would be marvelous."

"What a bold boy you are! Let me think about it."

"So, you agree. Quickly, let's get ready."

"Well, all right, but we first have to inform the King about our project."

"Mentor, please, let's keep it a secret."

"Ha, ha, ha."

Tobio was taken aback as he looked for the intruder who was laughing at him. All he saw was a black bird that flew away snickering.

"Don't be surprised, my boy, that bird always shows up when you talk about the Supreme Being."

"Well, I'll be!"

For the rest of the day the two explorers made preparations. The sectaphore was stuffed with all kinds of things. Sirius looked more like a soldier than ever in his green leather outfit. Tobio was dressed in his scout's uniform, but his bulging pockets ruined the elegance of his form.

"You've got too much stuff in your pockets, Tobio."

"Things of primary necessity, mentor. String, sling-shot, stones, a utility knife, flashlight, some hazelnuts, a pencil and notebook..."

"Are you planning to write?"

"I might need to draw maps. In any case, the notes I wrote on the first page will come in handy."

"What do they say."

"I'll read: What you think, you become. And: If we were always aware of the presence of God, we'd never be in danger."

"What else?"

"That's all."

"But I see more writing."

Tobio blushed. "I have to admit, mentor, that on Earth I had to battle against boredom. I was full of bright ideas and brave decisions, but I never went through with them. My mother kept repeating to me, hopelessly: It's not enough just to think, Tobio, you have to act or you'll never get anywhere. One time when I was even more slug-gish than usual, she translated something of Goethe that she was reading, then I wrote it in my notebook. Here it is:

"Are you sincere? Seize this very minute. Whatever you can do or dream, start it. Daring consists of genius and magic power. Action needs to be taken to kindle the spirit. Begin the work and it will be done."

"Indeed, Tobio, the key is there: BEGIN."

"So, let's go, mentor, let's begin."

The sectaphore rose slowly, took wide turns, then shot off and disappeared.

"Say, mentor, I still haven't seen the famous magic circles that surround the Land of the Fays."

"You can't see the invisible, Tobio. In fact, it's an aggressive fluid that repels anyone harboring bad feelings against the Good and the Beautiful. The King is immediately informed of the unwelcome visitor and gets ready to receive him."

"I can't understand why it wasn't suspicious of the Gray Wizard."

"I should add that the circles are lifted every afternoon when the King gives audience."

"Now I understand. Oh, mentor, look! That's funny!"

"It's the domain of the sprite Kooky. His castle is really good for a laugh. I'll get lower so you can see better."

Hundreds of paths covered with colorful gravel led to a huge building that was every shape and every color imaginable. In front of the house, in a hammock stretched between two trees, as tall as poplars, a fat man was lounging. He saw them coming and waved his short arms and squealed. Then, from all directions, dwarves and sprites, bunches of pixies, troops of gnomes and all kinds of animals sauntered forth.

"Mentor, let's go down there! It should be fun!"

Sirius took the sectaphore very low, leaned to the side and waved. "Can't do it, Tobio, we should never get diverted from our goal."

"You're right," Tobio sighed.

Soon some tall, rocky, bald mountains appeared.

"Here we are in the Land of the Yellow Dwarves. They're the least friendly of their kind. They never mix with the others and have many secrets. On that great plain yonder are the Iron Wizards, called this because they are always dressed in metal. They're the most loyal, but also the most stubborn, of wizards."

Night had fallen now and Tobio and his mentor took turns sleeping. Daybreak found them over a vast desert that extended far into the distance.

"It's pretty monotonous here," Tobio uttered.

"It only looks that way, my boy. If we landed, we'd soon be the playthings of unthinkable adventures because this desert is just a giant field of traps, the front line of the Supreme Being. See that wall on the horizon? You want adventure, Tobio, we're going to have plenty."

"Have you been here before, mentor?"

"Only once. I had to go back after spending a week of useless efforts trying to cross that wall. I first tried to fly over it. At 32,000 feet, the highest my machine could go, the wall was still there, going up into infinity. Then I tried to skirt along it in both directions. A wasted effort. There's no end to it."

"And who did you meet during this time?"

"Not a soul, human or animal. Oh, yes, when I started out, that famous black bird was determined to mock me."

"If he does it again, he'll be sorry, mentor."

Sirius landed near a grove of trees and while he hid the sectaphore Tobio walked up to the wall with his sling-shot at the ready.

"You'll have to surrender, stubborn wall," he said aloud.

"Ha, ha, ha," a jeering cry replied.

With narrowed eyes Tobio spotted the animal, pulled back his arm and aimed. The small rock hit its target and the bird fell. He picked it up, still warm and twitching. Its wounded wing was bleeding.

"What are you doing there, Tobio?"

"Just looking at my handiwork, mentor, and I'm not proud."

"Aye!" Sirius cried out when he saw Tobio trying to bandage the wing with his handkerchief.

"I'm really sorry for what I did! Mentor, can you heal him?"

"I'll try. Give him to me."

But as Tobio was momentarily letting go of his grip on his victim, it opened its wings and flew away.

"That makes me happy, but look what's in my handkerchief. A tiny silver hammer. What could this mean?"

"I think it's the key to the wall, my boy."

"Oh, that would be marvelous. Let's try it."

Tobio ran to the wall and hit it with his hammer. A crack appeared, which got bigger and bigger until the two adventurers could slip through easily.

They were on a big field full of all kinds of colorful and odd-shaped flowers. Merrily babbling brooks ran everywhere under branches of tall trees from which hung delicious red fruit.

After walking for a full hour they came to a black, wild chasm at the bottom of which were hideous, swarming monsters. It was at least five hundred yards wide.

"Second obstacle, mentor. Luckily, it's not uncrossable."

"Do you plan to use that narrow bridge over there? Have you noticed that it's so narrow you can't even put your feet together on it."

"Sure, but one before the other."

"Indeed. What do you think of the pretty beasties down below?"

"Let's read my second note again and then turn the verb 'begin' into an active form."

"Very well, Tobio. And let's add that when the path is drawn, even if it's dangerous, you have to take it bravely and confidently, ignoring the chasm to concentrate on the goal."

"So let's go. I'll go first."

One foot in front of the other, Tobio advanced slowly, keeping his balance with his arms held out on each side. To cover the noises of the monsters he repeated his note aloud. He was restarting it for the eleventh time when he reached the other side.

"I can tell you, mentor," Tobio said as he collapsed in the grass, "that I didn't find that very fun."

"Me neither, Tobio. In truth, it wasn't really dangerous because I could've protected you from a fall."

"Why didn't you tell me? You could've saved me from a harrowing ordeal."

"I wanted to test your bravery and faith."

"So, are you satisfied?"

"More than you could imagine."

"Me too, I'm happy I pulled it off. I'll be even happier if we can get the potion. What else do you think we'll have to do to find the Supreme Being?"

"As for that, Tobio, I'm afraid we'll never get there."

"You're right," a voice responded. "Nobody can see or get near the Supreme Being, but he is always near you and knows what you're thinking. Young man, because you're loyal and courageous you'll receive the potion you desire. Go look for it in that tree."

The voice went quiet. In the strange calm that followed, pleasant music filled the air. Tobio and Sirius waited excitedly in the exquisite environment.

"Hey, hey, hey!" the bird called out from the tree.

Tobio ran over. The branches were easy to climb and he was at the top in no time. He had to hold on tight with both hands to keep from falling when he saw the remarkable view. Far away, beyond a hill, was a palace of pure crystal, sitting on a pink, quivering cloud. Adorable little angels with shimmering wings were fluttering around and preening themselves.

"Mentor," Tobio shouted but the vision had already disappeared. On a leafy branch he saw a small, black vial all by itself. The cap looked like a diamond.

"What is it, Tobio?"

"I've got the potion," he said and clambered down the tree. "Look."

"Very good, my boy. First of all let's thank the Supreme Being for this kindness and then we'll go."

The two adventurers got back to the sectaphore very quickly since all the obstacles had disappeared. Sirius was surprised that Tobio was keeping so quiet. He asked him about it.

Tobio sighed, "At the top of the tree I saw the palace of the Supreme Being, mentor, and it was so wonderful that I'll dream about it for the rest of my life until I can get there some day."

"What a creature of Earth you are!"

CHAPTER X
With the giants and the Great Spirit

"I feel like we're going in the wrong direction, mentor."

"Well, we're not going back to my domain before going to the Great Spirit, Tobio."

"Good. Is it far?"

"At the other pole. At the speed we're going, we'll get there in a few days."

"What a weird bunch of mountains down there. It looks like there are huge blocks moving among them."

"Keep your eyes open, my boy, we're in the Land of Giants. What you think are mountains are actually their houses and those moving blocks are the giants. If you're nice and polite, they're gentle and generous. We'll have to land to pay our respects to their king."

"Marvelous! But what will happen if we don't stop?"

"One of the giants will catch us in his hand like we would do a fly and he'll crush us."

"You forget that we're not an insect but daring detectives."

"Well, my boy, for once in your life, you'll be able to know what is it like to be a microbe. A good experience to put your vanity and pride in its proper place."

"I'm surprised there are still others living on this planet if these giants are as powerful as you say."

"Powerful, but peaceful, Tobio. All the other races agreed to give them a vast territory that they can't leave. They accepted and live happily within their boundaries. But here we are over the royal palace. I'll go right in and land near the throne."

After diving through a gigantic door and zigzagging through countless hallways, the sectaphore made a wide turn to enter a huge room, all red marble and decorated with white flowers. In the middle of the room, on a throne the size of a hill, sat the King of the Giants. Tobio couldn't get over it. He'd always believed that the giants were double the size of a normal human, but this one was a lot bigger. His mentor, who was pretty tall, didn't even come up to his knees.

When he bowed, Tobio blushed, feeling so tiny and ridiculous.

The King howled a brief order, all in vowels, "Iua!"

Right away, a giant swept them up delicately and carried them up to the King's ear.

Cupping his hands around his mouth Sirius yelled, "Since we had to cross over your territory, Majesty, we came to pay our respects and ask for your protection in your land."

"Granted," the King roared.

Then to his subject who was holding the two detectives as if they were fragile little worms, he ordered, "Eou Iae!"

The giant put the tiny humans gently back into their machine. Tobio, who was almost breathless in his daze, fell headfirst into the back of the sectaphore. By the time he crawled back into his seat, they were already in the air.

"I'll never come back to this infernal land, mentor. Did you see how the monsters were making fun of us?"

"You were imagining it, Tobio. Tomorrow I'll take you to the marmosets. Their king, who is the biggest man in their land, is barely eight inches tall. I'll bet you that you won't be making fun of them, but you'll feel embarrassed and awkward around these miniature creatures."

"Maybe so, but at least it'll be fun and friendly. These giants are annoying and insufferable."

"Come on, my boy, eat some pie and buck up. Don't be humiliated by the adventure. Instead, consider that the poor giants are basically abnormal. Would you want to be like them?"

"Not at all! You're right, mentor, this pie is a ready cure for the doldrums. Since we're out of the nightmarish land, let's enjoy the good things of a normal life!"

"Eating and sleeping, the two main concerns of the people of Earth. Don't fear, my boy, I'll get you a nice, soft bed for the night."

"Hurrah! After that I'll even let one of your giants examine me with a magnifying glass."

"In any case, they'll be in your dreams. But we're there! See that square building, it's the Open House. Every passer-by can enter, eat and spend the night there. It's all done by magic. Tables are set and beds are made all by themselves. The sorcerer Nimbus set it up. He spends his time doing nice things for others."

"Will you introduce me? I love people like that."

"And rightfully so," Sirius agreed as he landed.

The two travelers sat in a bright room full of flowers at a table that was quickly covered with their favorite foods. However, when night fell, Tobio felt his eyes tingling and thought about the stories of the sandman that his mother used to tell him.

"Don't you worry, my boy. Go on and get into that soft bed that's just waiting for you."

How nice it was to lay down, stretch out, then fall asleep under a warm quilt! Tobio entered the land of dreams with a smile on his face...

"Get up, sleepy head! You'd sleep for days if I let you!"

"I don't think so, mentor. My nose would've certainly told me that good food was being served. Are we going to visit the marmosets today?"

"Yes, but quickly because even though they won't say anything, visits from such big people can't be very nice for them."

A few hours later, Tobio and his mentor were in sight of the Kingdom of the Marmosets. On a vast plain they saw a large collection of cute round huts with brightly colored roofs in the middle, teeming with busy, bustling little people.

"Oh, mentor, let's stop! I really want to see them up close!"

"Very well, but be careful where you walk."

All the marmosets ran away at the approach of the intruders. Here and there a scrunched up face appeared at a window or peeked out from behind a tree that only reached up to Tobio's waist.

"Mentor, look!"

In the middle of the road two children had stopped playing to watch worriedly as the two "monsters" came closer. Tobio picked them up gently to examine them. They were soft and limp, like baby birds. When they started bawling and struggling, he let them go and put a piece of bright and shiny silver from Earth next to them. The two kids were stunned by this new toy and knelt down to get a good look at the head and the decorations in relief on the round piece of metal.

Then all the bells started tolling and at the end of the road, on a chariot drawn by seven white mice, the King was approaching with his copious entourage. He stopped in front of the two visitors who bowed deeply.

"Majesty," Sirius spoke as softly as he could, "don't worry, we don't plan to stay long. We just came to pay a friendly visit."

"And to bring you fruit from Earth," Tobio took the hazelnuts out of his pocket.

"Thank you for the gift, but I'd be grateful if you put your plans to leave into effect immediately because my people are scared."

While the marmosets carefully carried the hazelnuts back to the palace, Sirius and Tobio walked gingerly back to the sectaphore. The entire city came out to see the fabulous machine as it took off and disappeared in the sky.

"Lucky my sister wasn't with us," said Tobio. "She wouldn't have resisted the temptation to grab a few of those living dolls. Are we going to be passing through other interesting lands?"

"Many, but we won't stop again. I'll describe as best I can when we fly over them."

After two more days of travel, Tobio saw a gigantic fortress on the horizon. Hundreds of towers and turrets stood out, all white, against the deep blue sky. When they got close, a huge drawbridge lowered and as soon as they reached it, they heard a low rumble as the main door slowly opened.

Sirius and Tobio, without saying a word, entered a round hallway whose walls were set with sparkling sapphires while countless golden stars twinkled in the ceiling. At the end, they saw the entrance to a room carved out of diamond. An opal throne stood in the middle. On the ground, out of the fresh, splendidly green moss, sprang lovely rosebuds that filled the air with their scent.

Sirius walked reverently up to the throne and poured the potion on the seat. Right away a majestic old man garbed in light appeared. The room was filled with sub-lime, diaphanous beings.

The Great Spirit raised his hand and his face lit up with a smile so sweet that all the roses opened their buds to look upon it. Tobio thought he was in heaven.

"A pleasure to see you, Sirius, because you are wise. When you have finished educating your ward, come back here and I will teach you everything I know. As for you, child of Earth, you are on the right path to become a man, but be careful of the fault that afflicts the adults on your planet—pride. Nobody has the right to be proud of what he is or what he does because it does not come from him but from God."

After saying this, the Great Spirit, the fortress and everything inside it vanished before the eyes of the two detectives. Tobio was trembling with emotion.

"That was incredible, mentor! And to think that I'm the only person from Earth who has seen anything like it. I bet that when I tell people about it, no one will believe me."

"It doesn't matter, my boy. What matters is that you've seen it and experienced it. Let's go back now to our domain where many more wonders and adventures are awaiting us."

HÉLÈNE GISIGER

TOBIO
DÉTECTIVE
AU PAYS DES FÉES

A NEUCHATEL
AUX ÉDITIONS DE LA BACONNIÈRE

TOBIO, DETECTIVE IN THE LAND OF THE FAYS

CHAPTER I
The Elegant

It was over a year ago that the sorcerer Sirius, Tobio's mentor on Jupiter, had gone to stay with the Great
Spirit. He had left his ward with his magnificent domain,
solid grounding in wisdom and a summary, in a big book,
of all his knowledge about the different people of the
planet.

After a thrilling ride on the son of Aster, Sirius's favorite mare, Tobio went to rest in the shade of the tall pine
trees that scented the air in front of his house. His friend,
the dog Fax, was lying at his feet while Mischief, his
small, white, angora cat, brought over her whole family.
The kittens were so funny, so soft and sloppy as they
teased and frolicked that even Fax seemed to curve his
jowls into a smile.

Tobio had never felt happier. He had just been publicly congratulated by the King of the Fays for the bravery
and intelligence he used in the tricky case of the Wizard
King Ramines X. The King was calling on him more and
more often to deal with serious problems in his realm so
that Tobio was now considered by the whole planet not
only as a daring detective, but also as the King of the
Fays' prime advisor. On the one hand, the fays, sorcerers,

dwarves and sprites loved him, but on the other hand, the wizards and other mean people were starting to fear him.

Ramines X and his cronies had decided to get rid of the Earth boy once and for all, because he had become friends of the good and the champion of the weak on Jupiter. To do this, they had organized a big competition of horse racing, archery and other games of skill in which they had set a bunch of traps to get Tobio killed. The "little king", as everyone had now nicknamed him, was an enthusiastic athlete, so he didn't want to miss the chance to win the games on behalf of the King of the Fays.

On the appointed day Tobio accepted the invitation, as the wizards had figured he would, and went to Ramines X' castle. On his beautiful roan horse, dressed all in green, followed by his dog, he looked very dashing. With his head held proudly high, his fearless eyes, his strong chin, tanned and strong, he stood out among the wizards who were deformed by their vices and wickedness.

Soon after his arrival all the guests sat down for the welcome. The meal was delicious and Tobio, a good eater, was more focused on the dishes they served than on the people around him. But after eating enough, he got a little startled by the person sitting on his right. He was a young sorcerer dressed with unusual elegance in blue silk. His soft, white hands wore many rings and the strong scent of daffodils wafted off his body. At that moment, the young sorcerer took a lace handkerchief out of his pocket and brought it casually up to his mouth to cover his bored yawn. When Tobio caught his gaze, he was surprised to see in his eyes an intense energy and a glimmer of mild mischief.

"I've wanted to meet you for a long time," he said to Tobio. "Since the first time I heard about your feats, I've wanted to be your friend and help you."

"That's very kind of you," Tobio replied, "but even though I know how to fight, to defend a good cause and play all kinds of sports, I know nothing about fashion and I hate perfumes and jewelry. What would happen to your pretty lace in a boxing match? Would your silk clothes last long riding horses across the lands?"

"I don't think you should judge me by my looks. I'm sure I'd prove worthy of you. Like you, I have no friends. Let's be friends and we'll be stronger together to do great things."

"I'll think about it," Tobio said kindly with one last discreet scowl at the lace handkerchief that the young man pulled out of his pocket for at least the tenth time.

"Please, everyone present," Ramines X stood up to announce, "let's all go into the park where the games will begin with a horse race. I have to tell you that the Iron Wizard will be racing for me on Satan. He's unbeatable and has all the odds to win the prize, which is an invisible shield that's been among my treasures for a thousand years. The race will be two and half miles in a straight line with six obstacles. Every horse has to stay in its lane matching the color of its rider. The two sides of the track are reserved for the wizards and fays, the middle is for everyone else."

Tobio, on Red Arrow, his fiery steed, took his place on the left side of the track, marked with gold. He was eager to see if he could beat the Iron Wizard. He had to win, but who would help him? Then his mouth dropped open when he saw his table-mate prancing over on a magnificent white horse.

"Hey, Elegant," he said, "do you want to help me win?"

"Absolutely, little king."

A whistle blew and the horses took off.

After the fourth obstacle, Elegant brushed by his partner and cried out, "We've caught up to the Iron Wizard. I'll drop out and you take my place. Whatever you do, don't hold back."

"I figured he wouldn't last until the end," Tobio muttered to himself. "It's probably his clothes that got in his way."

But he followed Elegant's advice. The Iron Wizard was whipping his horse and getting ahead.

Tobio leaned forward, patted his horse's neck and urged him on, "Buck up, Red Arrow! Giddiup! Don't let him pass us!"

The horse charged, caught up to Satan and after clearing the final obstacle as if he had wings, he crossed the finish line first.

The fays exploded with excitement, throwing flowers from their hair at the winner. The sorcerers clapped loudly and the dwarves whooped and wailed. Ramines X, pale and with a cruel glint in his eyes, presented Tobio with the invisible shield. The little king rushed over to give his prize to the King of the Fays.

"Congratulations and thank you in the name of my people," the monarch said when he hugged Tobio. "But keep the shield, you earned it."

"Thank you, Majesty," Tobio answered, thinking of something else. He had just remembered Elegant. Why did he give him advice?

As soon as Tobio managed to wriggle out of the crowd congratulating him, he went back to the track to get a look at the last and then next-to-last obstacle, which was a ditch filled with water. As he stepped up to the edge, the ground suddenly gave way and he fell into a deep hole.

"Yuck, disgusting!" he roared.

"No harm done," a casual voice said. "Grab the end of this rope."

Pulling himself out of the ditch, flushed with anger, Tobio couldn't help laughing when he saw Elegant calmly dusting off the dirt from his clothes.

"Sorry and thanks. You're an ace, Elegant. Let's be friends."

Leather sleeve hooked around silk sleeve, our two heroes went back cheerfully to the playing field where the archery competition had already started. Everyone could participate. So far it was a red dwarf who was excited to be holding the record. All the other dwarves, perched on the low branches of the trees, were patting their caps or holding onto their nervous bellies. Their champion had shot a hazelnut off the top of a pine tree at a hundred yards.

Tobio had excellent eyes and was an expert shot, but he hesitated to compete. Surely, nobody could do better than the dwarves and they were so happy, so proud of possibly winning the prize, a magic vase.

Elegant saw what his friend was thinking and smiled, "Generosity doesn't spoil courage, Tobio."

"True, Elegant, but still, if you were as good at archery as I am, you'd understand my hesitation."

Elegant didn't answer. He had just seen a bow, hidden in the trees, that was aiming at Tobio.

"I'm not a bad shot either, watch."

The arrow shot off and dropped to the ground not far away. Tobio laughed and went to pick it up but he was amazed to see that Elegant's arrow was stuck in the shaft of an ugly, sharp, black arrow.

"I don't understand!"

"But I do, little king. See that skinny wizard running into the forest? Can you believe that he was shooting at you?"

"Do you know what advice the Great Spirit gave me when I saw him with my mentor?"

"No."

"He warned me against pride, one of the great flaws of the people of Earth. I'm ashamed to have given in to it twice today already. So, instead of thanking you vainly for saving me again, I'll promise you to overcome this weakness."

"Very well, friend. Let's not talk about it anymore and let me take the two arrows to Ramines to show him that you, too, have allies."

"You're right to use the plural, friend, because with all respect to the silk and lace, you're worth ten men. From now on, I promise, I'll stop judging people by how they look. But the games are on again. Tell me the rules quickly so I can sign up."

"Well, this game has two parts, attack and defense. If you choose your opponent, you get to attack for ten minutes. If you haven't put him down by then, you lose. After a five-minute break, you start again but you're on defense. You can't use your hands. Oh, I see you won't have to go looking for an opponent. The Yellow Wizard, known for his savagery, is picking you as his opponent. Do you accept?"

"Me, pass up an opportunity to make a meany bite the dust? What do you think?"

"Be careful, this guy's as strong as he is sneaky."

"All the more reason for me to see if I remember my jujitsu, a famous method of defense on Earth, which a friend of mine taught me. When you've seen me use it, you can ask me for lessons."

As the sneering wizards looked on, their ruthless representative lunged at Tobio who dodged him nimbly. After a short time, with the wizard already panting with rage and wasted efforts, Tobio let him come close and then grabbed him in such a way that the opponent howled in pain, doubled over and dropped to the ground, then he turned over and lay on his back with his opponent's side cheering frantically.

As soon as the break was over Tobio got his scout's punch ready, stepped up to his adversary and socked him hard on the jaw. The brute's teeth were knocked loose and he fell down hard. He started seeing so many stars that the ten minutes passed without him moving a muscle. Tobio was the winner.

The fays, sorcerers, sprites and dwarves were overjoyed. But Tobio, afraid that all the cheers would fan the flames of his pride, went home, bringing his new friend with him.

"Well, little king, with your famous fighting method we have nothing to fear. You have to teach me and I swear we'll even be able to conquer the monster that's ravaging the Land of the White Dwarves."

"A monster? Come on, tell me everything. Is it a man or a beast?"

"I don't really know since I've never seen it. Luckily, because if you see it once, it'll never stop haunting you. Your hair turns white, your skin wrinkles, you get grouchy and lose all your joy and courage."

"How awful! Elegant, it's our duty to destroy it. Let's go get some rest so we can start the expedition tomorrow. Here's your room. I'm sorry I don't have silk sheets and fur carpets for you. Good night."

CHAPTER II
The monster

Using the sectaphore, the prized vehicle that the sorcerer Sirius had left to Tobio, our two friends arrived early the next day in the Land of the White Dwarves. It was a vast country with lots of pleasant lakes and mountains. It was a beautiful day, the sun was shining, the birds singing, the air was light.

"What a wonderful place!" Tobio smiled. "I wish I had wings like that skylark singing merrily in the sky so I could fly up and thank the Creator of all this beauty."

"Not everyone thinks like you, Tobio. Look at that man coming down the road. He looks pretty grim and gloomy."

"Maybe he's blind."

"No, he's a victim of the monster."

"What do you mean?"

"From what I know, when the monster attacks someone, it casts a kind of spell to keep the person from seeing the present. People will only see the future and they see it as dark."

"Really? Let's go find out from him."

Tobio approached the stranger and greeted him politely. Then he said, "Oh, you must be so happy to live in a land like this."

The man sneered at him and snapped, "Another crackpot from the Land of the Fays, I guess. They only know how to babble at the stars, gasp at stupid dandelions and kneel before the sun. You have no idea what life is."

"Life, Sir, is God, therefore harmony, beauty, joy and health."

"What about work? What do you do for work?"

"Work is the first law of Heaven. Working for the good of everyone is a pleasure."

"Pretty words! Too bad you don't practice what you preach! You don't look very busy, you know?"

"If I were a mason, I'd be whistling while building a house. If I were working in the fields, I'd be as happy as a monarch. But I'm a detective and for my work all I need are my smarts and my fists."

"Ho, ho! And why did a great detective come here?"

"To destroy the monster that's ravaging the land."

"Ha, ha, ha! A monster! Listen to him blubbering! A monster! I guess you've at least got a magnifying glass to find this marvel? Always searching for fantasies! Goodbye and good luck, great detective!"

"Goodbye. The next time we see each other you'll still be laughing but with joy!"

But the man was long gone.

"Say, Elegant, are all the white dwarves like that?"

"Most of them. Always in a bad mood, always worried about tomorrow. They like counting their money and saving it. They're selfish, never caring about their neighbors. They're afraid of sickness and are convinced that the air is infested with microbes that want to harm them. Listen to that mother over there telling her son to stay away from anyone who coughs."

"Let's go ask her if she's heard of the monster?"

"Hello, what a lovely child!"

"True, but so fragile. I'm always afraid of him catching cold, tripping and falling, all sorts of things can happen."

"But why? He'll be perfectly safe and sound if you trust in God."

"Maybe, but I can't help being afraid."

"Poor woman, what a horrible life to live in fear. I'm going to free you from it. Have you heard anything about a monster?"

"Yes, when I was little. An old dwarf who everyone thought was crazy used to say that on Black Mountain there was a deep cave where it lived. He used to claim that the thing had a harmful effect on the land."

"Where is this Black Mountain?"

"Behind you. That big, dark, barren mountain."

"Thank you. We're going to see if the story has any truth to it."

"Don't do it! You'll get hurt!"

"Goodbye and please, have no fear."

As they started climbing up the slope of the famous mountain, Tobio looked at his companion and smiled. "My word, Elegant, you look like the King in person with all your silks. I hope they don't get ruined on the climb. It's a good 6500 feet to the top and the last 1500 are pure rock."

"So you won't worry, little king, I'll put on my leather coat."

"You've got funny taste, Elegant. Red buttons on green leather, I never would've thought of that!"

"Don't tease me, Tobio. Instead, tell me stories about Earth."

While talking, our two heroes reached the foot of the rocks that shot straight up to the sky.

Elegant frowned, "This doesn't look possible. What do you think?"

"Possible with my rope. Look, I make a slipknot at one end, toss it over that spur up there and then climb. A detective's way. Follow me."

The two companions had gone only six or seven hundred feet when they heard a grinding noise to their left.

Since they had taken the precaution of covering the soles of their shoes with rubber, they could walk without making a sound. They stepped around a granite boulder and were surprised to see, farther on, through a crack, the entrance to a cave.

In front of the cave sat the most frightening creature they'd ever seen. His two long, skinny legs were bent beneath him. Ten dirty gray arms like tentacles dropped around his skeletal body. His big, round, bald, blackish head had no nose and only one eye at the top. This eye jutted out of its socket eight inches high and spat out small, black bubbles that floated like snowflakes through the air and over the plain. One of them landed on Elegant's cheek but when Tobio tried to touch it, it disappeared.

"Does it hurt, Elegant?"

"Not physically, Tobio, but morally. It's a monster's thought. As soon as it touched me, it insinuated a bad mood, doubt and discouragement."

"How horrible! Don't give in to it! Your thoughts should be stronger because they're happy and healthy. Keep them on guard and fight off the enemy."

"Don't worry, little king. Oh, look, there are only two ugly, yellow teeth in that slit of a mouth, but they must have made the grinding noise."

"Elegant, we've got to wring its neck and stop the bubbles coming from its evil eye. Think of all the damage done by these millions of bad thoughts pouring down on helpless minds! Let's go!"

They were able to get right up to the monster without it making a move. Maybe it didn't see them?

"Put your eye back in place, you wretch," Tobio shouted.

"Gladly, poor, poor young man," the small, sad voice surprised the two detectives.

"Look, I'm not poor and I don't need your pity," Tobio answered.

"I admire you, doomed one, for being so stoical when you're going to die."

"Me, die! Are you kidding? What can you do against me?"

"I have no desire to hurt you! It's sad enough to see you so pale and weak and, alas, the unknowing victim of a terrible illness."

"Liar!" Elegant cried out and stepped forward. "Don't believe a word of what this demon says, little king. It's only trying to upset you, to unnerve you; it's too cowardly to defend itself in any other way. Let's push it onto the rocks down below. It can go back to the void from which it came."

"What's the use of these useless efforts to destroy me," the monster said softly. "I'll always be reborn. To destroy a plant, you have to pull out the roots. If you just pick off the flower, a new one will grow. That's what it's like with me."

"So, what do they call you?" Tobio asked.

"WORRY," the tinny voice said.

"Well then, Worry, we're going to rid the land of your influence," Elegant said and he threw the monster over the edge.

For a moment the monster hovered over the void and spun around. That was when the two friends saw that it was held by an elastic cord. But the weight was too much and it snapped, shooting back into the cave while Worry dropped out of sight.

"I didn't like that story of a plant, Elegant. I think we should explore the cave. What do you think it meant?"

"It meant that it was only the effect, and even if we destroy it, the cause remains. You're right, let's take a look."

They walked down the long, cold passageway for two hours without seeing anything but harmless bats. Then Tobio grabbed his friend's arm and said, "Elegant, look! Something moved."

"It's only a bunch of spider webs."

"There's something behind them. See, on the ground, the rope. I'm going to pull it."

Tobio pulled and pulled. Yards of rope piled up behind him and it kept coming. Suddenly he felt resistance.

"Hook my flashlight onto one of your buttons, Elegant, and help me."

The two detectives pulled with all their might on the rope. They heard creaking and sighs and, after one last tug, they pulled out a big, gray, hairy mass. It was a gruesome head of an old woman without a body but surrounded by a bunch of small roots as thin as hair and squirming around.

"Yuck! What's this doing here?" Tobio spurt out. Then he jumped back. "Watch out, Elegant, it'll prick you like rose thorns. Don't touch it. Shine the light on me, I'm going to set this monstrosity on fire."

"Mercy, good sirs, mercy. Let me live here alone in the dark. You've hurt me enough by killing my son."

"Hey, are you talking about Worry? Then who are you?"

"FEAR."

"Well, Madame Fear, tonight all the white dwarves are going to be free of your abominable spell because we're going to destroy you. Hey, Elegant, what's with her? She isn't moving."

"No, because she just became the victim of her own poison. She just died of fear."

"Hurray! Let's burn her anyway, just in case."

The two detectives waited for the monster to be turned to ashes before setting off on the way back. At the bottom of the rocks they lit a big fire of celebration. On seeing it, the sages went to the King of the White Dwarves to announce the good news.

"Majesty, the prophecy came true. Fire appeared on Black Mountain. Our people have just been freed of the horrible enchantment afflicting them."

"Ring the bells," the King replied, "and get all the people to welcome the saviors. Bring them to me in the chariot of honor so that I can reward them as they deserve."

CHAPTER III
Astrobus

It was the Prime Minister of the White Dwarves, a grim character bedecked in gold, who met the detectives when they arrived at the foot of the mountain. He asked them to follow him to his King who wanted to congratulate them.

With a cheering crowd that gathered around the royal escort, between two rows of soldiers dressed in blue and yellow striped uniforms, Tobio and Elegant followed the Prime Minister into a solid gold carriage drawn by six white horses. The interior was padded with deep blue satin studded with sparkling diamonds. Sitting comfortably, bouncing gently, Tobio almost dozed off while Elegant smoothed his lace sleeves and sprayed his ruffles with a flowery perfume.

After crossing a forest the team of horses turned towards a big, blue lake on the shore of which stood one of the most beautiful castles Tobio had ever seen. It was all made of white marble with slender columns and delicately honeycombed towers. All around grew masses of pink carnations and mimosas. On the steps of the main door stood the King and his entourage.

With his long beard, his white hair and his fur coat, the monarch was truly majestic and he had such kind, tender eyes that Tobio liked him at first sight.

"Come, fine young men, let me thank you and reward you for your bravery," he said as he held out his hand. When he spied the motto engrave on Tobio's belt—*Always Ready*—he added, "I knew who you were by the description given me by one of my friends: heavy velvet pants, pockets stuffed, a big belt with a knife in a leather sheath, a brown shirt with the sleeves rolled up and an honest but no-nonsense gaze. You're the famous detective of the King of the Fays, right? But who's your partner?"

"My friend, Majesty, is a sorcerer whose nickname is Elegant."

"And rightly so," the King smiled slyly.

"Under his silk shirt beats a noble heart and all that lace is covering muscles of steel," Tobio quickly added so that they wouldn't underestimate his friend.

"Yes, I see, a pair of mighty adventurers! You must be hungry after that climb. Come and eat and you can tell me all about it."

Tobio and Elegant entered a huge, pink room in which there was a long table full of fine food and flowers. Pretty female dwarves wearing violet crowns served the guests, as an appetizer, a small, juicy melon stuffed with walnut cream and chocolate. While Tobio, a good eater, dug in with pleasure, Elegant told the tale of their expedition. When he got to the description of the death of Worry, everyone clapped. The noise made the odd fellow with a bald, lumpy head sitting across from Tobio drop his spoon and splash cream all over his face.

"Ha, ha, ha!" the King guffawed. "Our Astrobus has come back down to the planet. Where were you, my friend?"

"Certainly, certainly," the frightened man replied.

"Gentlemen from the Land of the Fays, may I present to you Astrobus, the greatest dreamer of this realm. He's never where his body is."

"Certainly, certainly," the dwarf repeated, still eating but as he hadn't noticed the disappearance of his spoon, he was using his fork.

"Astrobus is cooking up a new invention," the King said. "You won't get anything out of him until he's finished it. My whole castle is full of crazy machines that spank automatically or distribute rewards, all sorts of things. Imagine, he even built a flying machine! He was so insistent that I try it with him that I finally gave in. I was sick for two days afterward and I swear I'll never do it again. His big dream is to build a metal dragonfly that can fly him from one star to another. That's why we call him Astrobus."

The King kept talking about him without Astrobus paying any attention. He just ate absentmindedly, sprinkling his vegetables with sugar and his cake with salt, completely lost in thought.

"It's weird," the jovial King went on, "some of my subjects have no ideas at all and Astrobus has so many that his head is too small to contain them all, so they're bulging out and forming those lumps."

Even though he was funny-looking, Tobio thought he seemed nice. He'd always had a deep respect for ideas and often wondered where they came from. He, too, was starting to daydream when the King's voice brought him back to reality.

"But it's time for your reward. Hey, pages! Go get my treasures."

Ten small dwarves soon came, each carrying a case made of precious wood. As soon as they were opened, a colorful shimmer glistened from the velvet interior. Everyone strained to get a look at the marvels—except for Astrobus, who was writing numbers in a notebook, and Tobio, who was watching him with great interest.

Elegant was transfixed by an opal as radiant as a spring morning and as mysterious as a summer night.

"I see you've got good taste," the King said, holding out the exquisite stone. "You won't find anything like it in your entire kingdom. Since it's my favorite, I'm especially pleased to offer it to you."

"But I can't accept it, Majesty."

"I'm giving it to you. Nothing is too good for the saviors of my people."

The he turned to Tobio and asked:

"And you, which of these jewels tempts you?"

"Which of these jewels?" Tobio repeated dreamily.

"Ha, ha, ha!" Elegant had a good laugh. "Sorry, Sire, I have to tell you that my friend hasn't yet learned all the poetry of a precious stone or of a rare perfume. Give him this wonderful sapphire, it'll go nicely with the slingshot and nuts deep down in his pocket."

"That's true," Tobio admitted sadly.

"Not everyone has to have the same tastes," the King stated kindly. "Maybe you'll find something among my collections. Let's go and see."

"Excuse me, Majesty," Tobio interrupted, "but night is falling and I'd like to get my sectaphore before it gets dark."

"Your what? Is it an animal?" the king asked.

"No, Sire, it's the vehicle that brought us here. We left it at the border."

"That's pretty far. If you want, Astrobus can take you in one of his machines."

"Nothing would please me more," Tobio smiled eagerly.

Less than five minutes later, Astrobus was at the door with his machine and Tobio, after a quick "See you later" to the King and Elegant, followed the dwarf who had come to get him.

Astrobus' lumps were sticking out of a kind of tor-pedo fitted with thick rubber cushions around the outside. Tobio opened the door and sat in the comfortably padded seat.

"Strap yourself in like me. It's safer," the driver said.

No sooner had Tobio fastened the belt around his waist than a hard jolt threw him back in his seat. And before he could sit himself upright an abrupt stop hurled him forward. Completely unruffled, Astrobus clutched the wheel and stared at the big thermometer that had suddenly filled up with red liquid only to empty a second later. Jolt after jolt, following the initial shock, Tobio realized that every time his companion put his foot on a big pedal, the machine lurched forward.

"Incredible machine," Tobio stammered. "What do you call it?"

"Um, engineering and chemistry are more interesting to me than names, you know. Um, do you really think it needs one?"

"Of course. Hup! Hup! would fit perfectly."

"OK then, that's what we'll call it. With two 'H's of course."

"Naturally. We can even add an exclamation point. Then sensitive passengers will be advised not to eat too much because Hup! Hup! puts stomachs through the wringer, you know. But tell me, do you have a lot of machines like this?"

"A few. My flying machine, for example, will be great when I've put the finishing touches on it. I found a way to make it silent and hover in the air."

"Marvelous! Does it lurch forward too?"

"Yes, and that's what bothers me. It needs to move smoothly."

"What do you use to power it?"

"Solar energy."

"No way! Listen, Astrobus, I've got a proposition for you. Do you want to become friends, partners even? There are already two of us, Elegant and I, who are champions of the weak on Jupiter. Your intelligence combined with our strength and courage would allow us to accomplish great things. You can come live with me and I'll build a huge laboratory for you. All day long you can create, discover, build whatever you want. My friend, the dwarves and I will help you if you want."

The machine stopped so that Astrobus, visibly moved, could take a large, red handkerchief out of his pocket and dry his eyes. At last, shaking hands, he muttered, "My dream, my hopes, all my desires! Oh, bless you, my patron."

"Your friend," Tobio corrected. "There, that's it. Leave Hup! Hup! and come see my sectaphore, which will make you admire its builder, the sorcerer Sirius, I'm sure. Astrobus, what would you say if I told you that my machine also uses solar energy and it moves smoothly? But it can't hover and isn't silent. Still, it drives on land as easily as it flies through the air."

"Is it possible?" Astrobus cried out. "Quickly, I want to see this marvel."

The long caterpillar was there, sparkling clean. One push on a button and the cover slid back, revealing a double row of comfortable seats.

"Let's get Hup! Hup! behind the sectaphore and you can sit next to me, Astrobus. Here we go. If I want to speed up, I just push the wheel a little and it's done. To slow down or stop, I press this pedal."

"Wonderful! And we don't even feel the bumps on the ground."

"That's right. I'll show you the thousands of tiny feet that keep it stable. Do you want to make it fly like a bird? Here, pull this lever and we'll rise up slowly."

"Oh, I'll be so glad to be your friend!"

"Me too, Astrobus. I'm Tobio."

"Well then, long live our friendship! Long live Tobio!"

The King and Elegant were still in the exhibition room when Tobio and his new friend arrived.

"Majesty," Tobio said, "didn't you say you wanted to give me a reward?"

"Certainly," the King replied. "Tell me what you want and it'll be yours."

"Well, give me Astrobus."

"Astrobus! I heard you were extraordinary, but this is unbelievable! But I'll keep my word and if Astrobus agrees, you can take him."

"I... I'll go pack my things," Astrobus said. "Thank you, Sire."

While Elegant controlled his burning desire to laugh, Tobio bowed before the King and said, "Majesty, from this day forward, I and my friends, Elegant and Astrobus, are at your service. If ever you need us, call and we'll come running. Would you like to see my sectaphore?"

The King was still marveling at the ingenious vehicle when Astrobus, wearing a small, round hat held on by two lumps and a frock coat buttoned crosswise, came with his arms full of packages, then left again, huffing and puffing.

The King laughed heartily and told his dwarves there, with nothing to do, to help their comrade. They ran off and came back loaded down. Tobio was scared. They could never fit all this in the sectaphore. It was already stuffed full!

"That's all now," Astrobus declared humbly before the narrowed eyes of Elegant.

"Don't worry," Tobio said, "a move is a move. Besides, I've got an idea. We'll stack it up and tie it to the sectaphore. It'll make quite a sight!"

Elegant said, "You mean we'll sit in the middle of it and risk it falling on our heads? We'll look like traveling clowns!"

"Not at all what I was thinking, my elegant friend. I alone will be the trucker. You and Astrobus can follow in the luxury sedan behind me. Go and get Hup! Hup!, Astrobus."

After bidding farewell to the King, Tobio drove off, chuckling quietly.

CHAPTER IV
The guard

The whole day passed after Tobio got back home but Hup! Hup! and its passengers had still not arrived.

After getting some rest, he helped his dwarves prepare the cozy pavilion that belonged to Mocco before he had left to go with Sirius. All of Astrobus' packages were put in the big exercise room on the ground floor. This was where Mocco used to try to work off the weight he'd put on by eating all day. And this was where Astrobus would now let his mind run free. Yes, in fact, it would be easy to change the room into a laboratory.

Tobio ran his fingers over the bulging packages trying to figure out what was inside them; for example this long, hard cylinder. He was about to give in to the temptation to open it when his head dwarf came running in and shrieked, "Oh, Miti Tobio, a beast in the sky! Come and see!"

Tobio wasn't surprised to see a big, winged, multi-legged spider lurching through the air. When it got over the house it started slowly descending. Soon the heads of Elegant and Astrobus were visible, sticking out of the strange machine whose twenty feet made of springs touched the ground and after bouncing a little, finally stood still and stiff.

"What happened, Elegant?" Tobio asked.

"Let me take a shower and change my clothes and I'll tell you all about it," Elegant headed straight for the house.

"Sorry for making you wait and maybe worry, friend Tobio," Astrobus said as he gently closed the door of his vehicle. "Elegant didn't want anything to do with Hup! Hup!. We were barely on our way when he started swearing and threatening to smash me and my machine to smithereens if I didn't go back right away. So, I did. Since it was already late, the King insisted we spend the night in the palace. When I got to my flying machine in the morning, it wasn't working well. I had to fix it and we couldn't leave until after the welcome."

"You know, Astrobus, that your machine looks thrilling me. I can't wait to try it out. But tell me, was Elegant more reasonable the second time?"

"He was a peach. To make the trip more comfortable I got some friends to help me line the interior with silk and set out some vases with carnations. I knew water would spill out of them with every jolt so I filled them with perfume. After the initial kick, he frowned but when he sniffed the heady scents tickling his nostrils, he smiled. Halfway through the trip he said, 'You're a good guy, Astrobus, and your machine isn't so bad after all. I have the feeling that the three of us are going to work well together.'"

"Bravo! Now you can come and eat something," Tobio was happy to learn that Elegant held no grudge against him for the little trick he'd played on him.

The two friends got to the table at the same time as Elegant, refreshed and spruced up in a white satin suit. Astrobus was feeling perky. In this simple, congenial atmosphere among friends who understood him, he found life beautiful. Elegant was a charming talker and Tobio spiced up the meal with laughter that was so contagious it seasoned all the food.

Only at dessert did Astrobus ask about his packages.

"Oh, they're here," Tobio assured him. "One of them, a long tube, really interested me."

"I see," Astrobus smiled, "it's probably my eye that brings things closer."

"So, a telescope?"

"If you'd like, Tobio. You have a knack for naming things. The telescope, the far-seeing, it fits well. You'll have to name my flying machine, too."

"Hey, sorry," Elegant cut in, "but it's me who'll name that machine, I'll baptize it! What do you think of the 'Fragrant Shock' or the 'Scented Jolt?'"

Astrobus stammered, "I think, I mean, maybe that's a little too mechanical. I'd like something with an 'h' and 'y,' that'd be nice."

"Phylomena," Tobio shouted.

"That sounds like a feminine name."

"Hurray! Exactly what's needed!" Elegant said. "The graceful Phylomena will be the friend of the long, rigid sectaphore and Hup! Hup! their cranky old uncle."

"A fascinating trio, just like us," Astrobus laughed merrily. "When are we going to unpack? You'll help me, won't you?"

"It'll be my pleasure," Tobio replied. He jumped up, his eyes sparkling with impatience.

When they left the house, all the windows were occupied by the faces of curious dwarves whose small, round eyes stared at the new friend of their master.

As they approached the new residence of Astrobus, Tobio told his companions about the funny spells that Mocco had put on it.

"Sorry I can't take you down the path of needles, it has a certain charm, I assure you."

"Your mentor and his friend must've been very formidable sorcerers," Elegant said. "Will you ever see them again?"

"One never comes back from the Great Spirit's house. But if I have to leave this planet someday to go back to Earth, you two can come say farewell."

"Is this really going to be my house?" Astrobus changed the subject because he saw that Tobio was getting sad.

"Of course."

"Oh, my friends, I'm going to be so happy! Where are we going to put our laboratory?"

"That's nice of you to say 'our'. Right here!" Tobio opened the door to the former exercise room.

"But it's huge," Astrobus was overjoyed. "Everything will have its own big space. Yes, I can work here! Where shall we begin?"

"Let's start by opening all the packages," Tobio suggested. "Elegant with his delicate hands can unwrap the delicate things and I'll go at the crates."

"Be careful not to damage Halthamyamus."

"Halthamyamus?"

"My guard."

"Astrobus, you're not telling us you wrapped up a man in one of these crates?"

"Yes, and until now, my best friend."

Tobio and Elegant frantically pulled out the nails on the top of the crate while Astrobus watched them with a mischievous gleam in his eyes. After lifting off the cover, the two detectives threw off the straw packaging and took out a black dwarf with hideous red eyes. His hair was made of iron and his fingernails of steel.

Tobio was astonished, "What do you use this toy for?"

"When I was living with the White Dwarves I only had one room at the palace. My many inventions, my works in progress piqued the curiosity of a lot of people.

I invented complicated locks for my door when I wasn't there, but all in vain. Someone had always got in and rifled through my stuff. Then I got the idea to create Halthamyamus and to tell no one about it. With my friend was born the legend that my room was haunted and I could work in peace. I'll show you what Halthamyamus can do. Keep unpacking while I set him up in a room."

For fifteen minutes Tobio and Elegant were alone. While talking about the weird Halthamyamus they had unwrapped everything and found an odd assortment of objects. There was a wand with the head of a serpent, the telescope, a big ear with a hole on one side and a thin sieve on the other, a pair of shiny skates, all kinds of boxes, containers full of unknown liquids.

"You can come in," Astrobus announced.

Tobio bounded over. Elegant took his time.

"See," Astrobus said, "I locked the door. Here, Tobio, open it slowly, cautiously, as if you were a thief. Don't put the key in all the way, wiggle it around a little, it's supposed to be a copy."

Tobio did as he was told.

He had barely stuck the key in when he heard a gloomy voice: "Come! Come! I'm waiting for you! I'll pluck off your head like a chicken feather. I'll rip out your teeth and make a necklace of them. Your eyes would make nice cuff-links. Come! Come! I'm getting impatient!"

"Oh, what a voice! What threats!" Elegant was doubled over laughing.

"Still," Tobio observed, "if you didn't know better and had come to break in, you'd be terrified hearing that. Watch out, I'm opening the door."

In the darkness of the room (because Astrobus had closed the shutters) stood a ghost with burning red eyes. Tobio stepped in but a ghastly cackle made him recoil.

"My word," he said, "I think I'm impressed."

He made a sudden decision to head straight for the supernatural being.

"Stop!" Astrobus shouted. "No need to go any further. Halthamyamus doesn't know his friends yet and if you get near him when he's on watch, he'll ruthlessly stab his steel fingers into you."

The nightmare disappeared with the sun.

Full of curiosity, Tobio asked, "Does it work all by itself?"

"No, you're the one that turned it on."

"How did I do that?"

"By putting the key in the lock you touched the wire that starts his voice. When you entered you stepped on a slat hidden under the carpet and connected to my friend. That started the cackle. Now, go on and see how he raises his arms and opens his fingers. If you get right up to him the springs will uncoil and he'll snatch up his prey."

"Incredible, Astrobus," Tobio exclaimed. "I have an idea! In the future, these houses will be our vacation homes. We're going to build a chalet on the mountain to work in. Outside will be all rustic and cozy but its location along with an internal defense system will make it fortress. Halthamyamus and other machines I'm thinking of will be the guards."

"All right," Elegant said, "but why on the mountain?"

"Because the air is refreshing, vivifying, which is good for the body and mind to work. Plus, we'll be overlooking the whole countryside around, which will give us both a strategic advantage and peace of mind."

"But we'll be far away from everyone else. Me, I like going to the balls and dancing tea parties they have on the big lawns of the castle."

"You'll be a big hit with the ladies, Elegant, when you come flying gracefully out of the sky in Phylomena or racing in with the sectaphore or mysteriously riding in the stunning Hup! Hup!."

"That's true, Tobio. You have an answer to everything. What do you think of all this, Astrobus?"

"I approve. If you'd like I can start tomorrow on plans for the chalet. On the ground floor we'll make a big living room, a kitchen and the laboratory. The bedrooms will be upstairs and there'll be a tower for a glassed-in observatory. From there you can try out my telescope. It cost me three lumps but it's better even than Halthamyamus."

"Astrobus," Tobio said, "you're without a doubt the most valuable person on the planet. Now let's go see the King of the Fays and ask permission to build on the mountain. We can take the opportunity to introduce you to him and all our friends. Get dressed for the occasion and we'll meet back here in fifteen minutes."

Elegant coughed, "Uh, excuse me, but let's say one hour."

CHAPTER V
Koullit the Prankster

When Tobio and his companions arrived at the palace, they were rushed to the King of the Fays who was meeting with his close friends, some fine sorcerers, in his personal sitting room. The monarch's face, usually so gentle and jolly, was serious. However, on seeing the newcomers his eyes lit up with joy and he jumped out of his chair.

"Tobio, at last, my wandering detective!"

"At your service, Majesty. Allow me to introduce my two partners."

"Aren't you the son of my friend Pagès?" the King asked Elegant.

"That I am, Sire."

"Refined," the King smiled, "and brave and loyal to boot. My compliments, Tobio, you chose your friends wisely."

"But Majesty, I didn't choose Elegant, he chose me."

"Ha, ha, Elegant! A nickname of yours, I imagine, and it fits him like a T. So, Elegant, you wanted to be friends with my detective? Either I'm sorely mistaken or you've got a taste for adventure!"

"Indeed, Majesty, I dream of nothing but mysteries to solve and dangerous expeditions."

"Well, I've got plenty to satisfy you. But what's your second companion's name?"

"Astrobus, Sire. He's a white dwarf gifted with extraordinary intelligence."

"Happy to make your acquaintance, Astrobus. And do you dream of nothing but lumps and injuries?"

"Oh, I don't like injuries much and as for the lumps, they're no dream, unfortunately, but very real."

"Indeed," the King agreed as the sorcerers joined in his laughter. "What projects do you have?"

"I'd like to build a machine even better than Hup! Hup! and Phylomena and a small army of automatons that will be stronger than Halthamyamus."

"Ha, ha, ha," the King laughed even more loudly. "One-of-a-kind! What in the world could you mean with such names?"

"Marvelous machines, Majesty. Our friend is an inventor. We came to ask for your blessing to build a chalet on one of your mountains. It'll be the headquarters for your detectives."

"I allow you not only to build it, but I'll give you the whole mountain if you help me solve a problem that's bothering me."

"We're ready."

Looking into the excited, determined eyes of his detectives the King started explaining the matter.

"You know that it's only through the use of patience and the strength of diplomacy that there's relative peace between my kingdom and that of the Wizards. Troublemakers and bigmouths, not a week goes by that Ramines X doesn't insult me, or that one of his subjects doesn't abuse one of mine. Right now, the Land of Wizards is in turmoil. Everyone is leaving their homes to camp out in the open in order to escape a sickness that hits them when they stay home. Their bodies and faces get covered with ugly red spots. They can't sleep at night because of all the itching and scratching. The first wizard who got the idea to set up a tent in his garden saw the redness disappear and the itching stopped completely. So, other victims of the sickness followed his example so that, right now, more than half the castles, including the King's, are empty. Their best men went out searching for the cause but found nothing. Yesterday Ramines X came to me and offered a year of guaranteed peace if one of us could solve this mystery."

During this speech Tobio struggled to stay serious. If it weren't for his respect for the King and the prospect of a year of peace, he would have willing left the mean wizards to their torment. But the story was kind of fascinating and it always felt good to help enemies.

Turning to Elegant with a playful grin on his face, he asked, "What do you think, Elegant?"

"Go help the wizards? It's nothing to sneeze at, for sure. I'm ready to give it a go."

"Me too," Tobio agreed. "Majesty, you can count on us. Very soon you'll have your declaration of peace signed by Ramines X in person, or I'll give up being a detective!"

"Go, then, my friends, and thank you. As a reward, the most beautiful mountain will be waiting for you."

Tobio told his partners on the way back, "First, we need to think, then act. While Astrobus is finishing up the plans for our fortress, you and I can go to study the wizards' problem."

"Good idea, Tobio. Let's drop Astrobus off at his pavilion and go directly to see the Wizard King."

At the entrance to his tent, arms crossed over his chest, his big cape fluttering behind him, Ramines X watched gravely as the two figures came down the path out of the forest. He was thinking: "Of course that big dope of a king came up with nothing better than to send me this hapless Tobio! I wonder whether it'd be better if we kept trying to solve this mystery ourselves, or just suffer through it, rather than owe our salvation to this insufferable Earthling?"

"Majesty, I'm honored to greet you and, along with my friend Elegant, to work with you to fulfill this mission that will result in a year's peace with my King and his people," Tobio said politely.

"A year's peace at the end of which they will all go soft in the head," the Wizard King snickered under his breath. "So be it," he continued aloud. "I accept! But on one condition: if you fail, you'll go back to your miserable planet, the Earth."

"Agreed, Majesty. One condition for me, too: if I succeed, you will publicly and honestly declare that an Earthling, with his bravery and intelligence, can sometimes be very useful on this great and noble world, Jupiter."

"Very well. And since you like compliments, hurry up and earn them. For as long as your investigation lasts, you can travel freely in my territory, visit the castles and interrogate my subjects."

"Thank you, Majesty, and our respects to you," the two detectives answered bowing.

But Ramine Xs had already turned away his stern eyes and gone back into the tent.

"What a delightful character," Tobio smiled sarcastically at his friend. "What if we went to his castle?"

"Let's go. We're already on the road leading to it."

Between two rows of trees as tall as poplars bristling with long, spiky leaves, the two young men walked towards the favorite residence of the King.

Suddenly Tobio grabbed his companion's arm and said, "Shh! Look at that little screwball sitting there on the wall. Have you ever laughed like that when you're alone?"

The little man hadn't noticed them and kept up his weird giggling. Sometimes he had to wipe his eyes and then he rubbed his hands together or mumbled something.

"I know him," Elegant whispered. 'It's the old sorcerer Koullit. I went nuts over him when I was a kid. He knew such fantastic stories and told them so well. He was the funnest and funniest man of the land."

"At least he looks nice with his pink, almost hairless, head and his cute cheeks, all round and red. What if we say hello? Maybe he'll tell us what's so funny."

"Oh, I know what it is. He must've played a joke on someone. It's his favorite hobby. Come on, I'll introduce you."

Hearing the footsteps on the path, Koullit turned his head and looked slyly at the two newcomers. "What a pleasant surprise," he said to Elegant. "I bet you still love stories, young man. Come and sit next to me because I've got a good one for you. And who's your friend? I can't say I've seen him before?"

"This is Tobio, the Earthling and famous detective of the King of the Fays. I'm sure you've heard of him."

"Of course! Glad to meet you, Tobio, you've got quite a reputation."

When Tobio, excited to meet this new character, shook the man's tender hand vigorously, Koullit grimaced.

"Aye! You've got a grip there! It could crush a wizard! Ha, ha, ha! Me, I demolish them with nothing but my ideas. Look at that pompous castle all empty. You should've seen brave Ramines X scampering out of there like the Devil was after him. His noble nose was covered in red spots and his white skin was blotchy. Oh, all these wizards were laughing when he called me a 'clumsy oaf' at a banquet. But it's my turn now. Sit down and I'll tell you about it. You're not in a hurry are you?"

"Well, we are on a mission. The King of the Fays sent us here to discover and destroy the cause of the epidemic that's thrown the wizards into a panic. If we succeed, Ramines X will sign a peace treaty with our land for one year. Maybe you could help us? With all your…"

But Tobio didn't finish when he saw the expression of utter amazement on the old sorcerer's face.

Koullit looked even craftier as he got all excited. He told the detectives, "Listen up, I'll name the guilty party."

Tobio was surprised, "What? You know who it is?"

"I know him very well… It's me!"

"You?" the two friends cried out together, not believing their ears. It was easy to guess what they were thinking: "The poor old guy has lost his marbles."

"Ha, ha, ha," Koullit guffawed. "You think I'm just babbling, don't you? Come with me to the castle."

Tobio and Elegant followed the sorcerer who kept talking.

"It was really just a little joke. I never would've thought it could turn out like this. The wizards believe that a terrifying sickness has afflicted them, or maybe that an invisible monster is haunting their land. We can't tell them the truth. The fear is keeping a lid on their meanness. Plus, it's a good thing that they've now learned to respect our brilliant detectives. That's why we have to keep the whole matter a secret. Promise?"

"Sure," the two detectives agreed, starting to believe that Koullit was serious.

In the castle the sorcerer took his companions straight into the Wizard King's bedroom. He bent down by the bed and from a hidden compartment in a piece of furniture he pulled out a small box and held it up.

"Here's where the monsters live! There are no less than a hundred of them. Maybe you know them, Tobio, because they come from Earth. An old witch, long gone now, brought them and she had fun training them. She gave them to me as a gift for a service I rendered for her. During the day, they're used to resting quietly in their house, but at midnight they come out through this little hole to feed, then they come back at dawn. Here, have a look," Koullit cracked open the cover.

"A nightmare! Fleas!" Tobio cried out. "Close it! Just seeing the dirty little creatures makes me itch all over. Wait, there's better things to do with them. Let's burn them! But I imagine you've got more somewhere?"

"You bet," Koullit answered proudly. "In nineteen castles."

"Koullit, I congratulate you, your joke was a great success, but believe me, it's gone far enough. Let's get started on destroying this vermin right now…"

A few days later Tobio and Elegant, along with old Koullit, who wanted to see the prank through to the end, went back to Ramines X.

"Majesty," Tobio announced, bowing with one hand on his chest, "our mission is accomplished. You and your subjects can go back to your castles. The 1900 monsters making them unlivable have been captured and burned alive."

"If all the inhabitants of Earth are liars and braggarts like you, it must not be much fun living there," the Wizard King sneered. "Still, I'll go back to my castle tonight, and if all is well in one week, I'll guess there's some truth to what you're saying. Since I always keep my word, I'll draw up the peace agreement and sign it with a declaration saying that I recognize the service done for us by an

Earthling. You can also appear before my Council of Ministers to explain the details of your exploits and the nature of this army of monsters."

"Thank you, Majesty," Tobio replied. "We'll tell our King that on the seventh moon, he will receive the signed treaty along with the declaration about me. As for bragging and lying, as you say, in front of your Council, you can forget about it."

Happy and smiling, the three friends went back to their land while Ramines X turned back to his castle, puzzled and curious.

Only the King of the Fays was told the details of the detectives' expedition. He had a good laugh and they all promised to keep it a secret. He was also so happy to see Koullit in his court again that he kept him there for several days.

The messenger from Ramines X came on time with the promised documents and Tobio received the proclamation, exquisitely engraved on a scented piece of bark, of the King of the Fays' gift to him of Dream Mountain.

CHAPTER VI
Dream Mountain

"While the dwarves are packing up our stuff, let's go visit Dream Mountain," Tobio suggested.

"All right," Astrobus replied, "I'll take Hup! Hup! with Halthamyamus, my telescope and a few other things."

"I'll follow in Phylomena and everything we'll need to stay clean and healthy," Elegant added.

"Great," Tobio said. "My sectaphore will take the tents, food and the tools we'll need to build the chalet. We can explore the area, make plans, then come back to get our dwarf friends to help us."

A few minutes later, the convoy set off. The long, supple sectaphore with its vital cargo glided through woods and over the prairies, followed by Hup! Hup! bouncing along merrily and Phylomena flying low, keeping them in sight.

Soon enough Dream Mountain appeared. It was a tall mountain with flowery slopes, thick forests and a treeless summit in the shape of a skull. A small, narrow valley separated it from the Land of the Wizards.

The odd convoy must have chased away all the creatures in the woods because Tobio saw nothing as they went through. At any rate, he was busy driving his big caterpillar on the easiest path for Hup! Hup!. Almost at the top, near one last grove of pine trees, he stopped. Veering gracefully in the blue sky Phylomena came down and landed at the very moment when Astrobus jolted to a stop.

"Oh, my friends," Tobio shouted, "isn't this the ideal place for us to build? To the south is the Land of the Fays, and to the north that of the Wizards. We can make out our King's palace over there, and on that big hill to the right must be the metal castle of Ramines X."

"You could see better with my telescope," Astrobus said softly.

"Great idea!" Tobio shouted again. "I didn't even think of your wonderful telescope. Show it to me, Astrobus."

Taking out of his pocket a handkerchief as big as a bedsheet, Astrobus used it to wipe the gray lens at the end of the long tube. Then he handed it to Tobio by the other end, which had three holes.

"Put it up to your eye while pressing the buttons on either side and it'll automatically adjust to your vision."

Tobio did as he was told and aimed the telescope at the Land of the Wizards.

He exclaimed, "This is fun! Elegant, you've got to see this! In his garden, sitting in the grass, I can see the terrible wizard Rabiès playing with his white rabbits. Hey, there's the entrance to Ramines' castle. What a break for us! We can spy on everything the enemies are doing without being seen by them. Astrobus, you've given us an edge. Elegant, take a look."

"Gladly because I'm curious to know if we can see our own place, Tobio. Ah yes, there it is. Oh, those dodgy toads! Do you know what they're doing? They're sticking their little noses in all my bottles. Little scamps! Close them up or they'll all evaporate!"

Elegant shook the telescope in the air and then put it back against his eye.

"Oh!"

"What is it?" Tobio was getting annoyed. "You've been standing here for five minutes with your mouth open and not saying a word."

"Unbelievable!"

"What? Come on, speak up!"

"Sorcerer."

"If you don't stop, I'll yank the telescope out of your hands," Tobio yelled. "What do you see?"

"On the west slope of our mountain, in the middle of a clearing, there's a tiny little, warm brown chalet covered in climbing roses and peculiarly beautiful flowers and a charming fay smiling at the weird flying creatures around her."

"Give me the telescope, Elegant, you're seeing things."

"Careful, Tobio, keep it in the same direction."

"Has your invention ever created mirages before, Astrobus?" Tobio asked after a moment of astonishment.

"It's the model of precision."

"Elegant, let's try to figure out where it is and go there at once."

"Wait!" Astrobus ordered. "My telescope has another use: it can calculate distances and the location of what it views. You just have to open it, slip this spindle into a special little slot, close it and look for the clearing. There, I've got it. I press this yellow button here in the middle, wait a few seconds, then remove the spindle. See what it says."

"Nothing at all."

"And these four mines coming down from the top and these two on the other side, is that nothing?"

"I don't see…"

"Obviously you don't understand how to use the spindle. Get into Phylomena and watch what I do."

Astrobus put the small object under the control panel where the altitude and speed were indicated. In the middle was a red disk that Tobio didn't know how to use.

Astrobus continued, "Now the spindle is in place and I'll spin the wheel that won't stop until we're over the clearing. Off we go!"

The long, transparent wings of Phylomena glittered in the sun and its graceful, gold body quivered with its three passengers as the springs unwound and poof... through the wild blue yonder!

Tobio kept his eye on the red disk that was swaying like the balance wheel in a watch. A click and Phylomena turned left, another and it went straight ahead, then the disk started humming and stopped. The flying machine landed in the clearing.

Under any other circumstances, Tobio and Elegant, being very polite, would have run up to the divine fay and paid their respects. Today, they were so stunned by what they saw that they couldn't move. Astrobus even forgot to rub his lumps, which he always did when he was baffled.

All around them were flying the most extraordinary and exquisite butterflies with tiny heads of women. One of them with wide, velvety, orange wings, alit on Tobio's hand. He could see the two bright, golden eyes in the minuscule face. Elegant was enraptured by the baby blue eyes and Astrobus flustered by the fiery green ones staring at him.

"Little ones," called a sweet voice before tinkling laughter rang out.

"Excuse me and greetings," Tobio walked with his friends over to the fay. "We're the detectives of the King of the Fays."

As they went together to the chalet, a bunch of the flying creatures vanished as if by magic in a desperate escape.

"They're my zizis, little wood sprites," the fay's gentle voice went on. "They'll come back. They're so curious."

"I never knew a place like this existed on our planet," Elegant blushed.

"Really, pretty sorcerer? But now that you know the Dream Fay and her enchanted clearing, I hope you'll come back."

Tobio saw nothing of his brave and remarkably cool-headed friend in this shy Elegant. So, without giving him time to respond, he asked the fay: "Are all these splendid butterflies also sprites?"

"No, they're dreams. Dreams I send to Earth every day."

"What a strange idea! Where do they come from?"

"At twilight I kneel down in the middle of my clearing and thank the Creator for all his bounty. Afterward, from my heart I take out thoughts of love, joy and gratitude. All the splendid flowers you see here receive one. Then the night is spent caressing them. The petals close up over the dreams that bloom. One drop of fresh dew, which the whimsical dawn drops on the sleeping butterflies in the morning, awakens them. And the rising sun sprinkles them with golden dust and light. Until noon my pretty dreams soak up the sweetness of the air, the splendor of the flowers, the harmony of the colors, the perfection of nature and the radiance of God and then they fly off, one after another, towards that pale, blue, distant star that is the Earth.

"Some arrive during the day, others at night. All of them rush to find a heart that weeps, suffers, hopes, desires, one with a small door open and that is tender. The dream lodges itself in this living hideaway and fills it with all its beauty and joy."

"Lady, you're the most useful magician there is and we're going to be happy to live near you. Isn't that right, Elegant?"

A rascally zizi had just put an end to the young sorcerer's bashfulness by falling into the glass of nectar he was holding. Everyone laughed and the impish little sprites reappeared everywhere. Being transparent, they took on the color of the object they landed on, camouflaged on the leaves of the trees. The merry murmur spread through the forest.

"I understand now why they call this Dream Mountain," Astrobus said. "I wonder if there's anything to be learned from this, yes, I wonder…"

"Our inventor is back to his old habits," Tobio smiled. "Lovely fay, we thank you warmly and bid you farewell. We have to go build our chalet near the summit. When it's done, would you come visit for its house-warming? That would be the best gift."

"With pleasure, my friends. Good luck and see you soon."

"Hey, Elegant, are you dreaming?" Tobio asked on the way back. "Do you realize that you haven't opened your mouth since we left?"

"It's because I've never seen such a beautiful fay."

"By Cupid, don't go falling in love on us! Think of our chalet, our projects, our coming adventures. Hurry, Astrobus, I want to get shovels in our hands as quickly as possible."

Their landing at the camp chased away a horde of squirrels, birds, hares and other curious animals that were sniffing, chattering and squawking at the sectaphore and its chubby partner. Under Tobio's expert command, the tents were pitched and while Astrobus was hammering down the stakes in the four corners of their future home, Tobio and Elegant prepared the meal.

"It's always better to work on a full stomach," Tobio declared. "What do think about going to get the dwarves in the sectaphore, Elegant? You can come back tomorrow at dawn and we'll finish digging the foundation. Make sure they all bring their tools. I'll keep working until nightfall."

"All right, Tobio, I'll leave right away. I can't wait to scold the naughty ones and to see what they did to my bottles. They're going to be knocked for a loop when I tell them we saw everything."

Soon after this, with his shirt off and his biceps bulging Tobio was swinging the pick and shovel with zeal. Astrobus, not such a novice at this new sport, was busy marking off the outline of chalet and the tall tower that would be added to it.

When a gallant, laughing moon appeared in the sky, Tobio put down his tools. Sweat was trickling down his forehead. He was tired but happy.

"Let's go to bed, Astrobus, and have dreams worthy of this mountain. Good night."

As Astrobus lay down, smiling, his head cradled in his arm, next to him all the little sprites and pixies and gnomes from Dream Mountain hustled and bustled around the ever-growing pit that was destined to be the fortress of the famous detectives.

CHAPTER VII
Hauroc

"It's really incredible," Elegant kept saying when he saw the work done since the day before. "I can see why Tobio's still sleeping."

As soon as they got out of the sectaphore, the dwarves went and sat on the moss in the shade of a pine tree and started whistling.

"Hey, friends!" Elegant shouted at them. "Did you forget that the song goes '*Whistle while we work*?' Come on, it's time to start the foundation. I don't have to tell you how to do it because you know very well."

Still whistling, the dwarves scattered around in search of rocks that they rolled back and using weird little saws with green teeth they transformed them into square blocks.

"Good grief!" Tobio cried out as he jumped up. "Why'd you let me sleep so long? I'll end up getting lazy!"

"Don't get yourself in a tizzy," Elegant said. "Digging the foundations in a few hours, incredible! I can't imagine how you did it."

"Tell me, Elegant, are you feeling all right?" Tobio sounded concerned. "Lay down for a minute while I go talk to the dwarves."

"No need to talk to them, Tobio, they know what they're doing and they'll finish the foundation before the welcome."

"You don't build the foundation on the ground, poor kid, you have to dig it out first."

"What? You want to dig even more?"

"But we have to. Come and I'll explain."

When they got to the pit Tobio gasped in astonishment.

"What's this, Elegant? Did you come and work during the night? I don't understand."

"Please stop joking with me. You know very well that this is your doing. Believe me, I appreciate your work and congratulate you, but let's be serious now."

"Well, Elegant, since neither you nor I dug this pit, there's only Astrobus. With all his inventions, I guess we shouldn't be surprised. Why didn't we think of it earlier? Where is he? Have you seen him?"

"No. Call out. Your voice is louder so he should hear it wherever he is."

"And my eyes are sharper so I can see a lumpy head sticking up at the top of that tree."

"Sure enough, Tobio, that's our friend. What's he doing up there? Hey, Astrobus? Have you got a pretty view?"

"Sure do, sure do," the dwarf stammered.

"Did you find something? Should we come up?"

"No, I'm coming down."

When the dwarf reached the ground with his head all scratched up, Tobio grabbed him by the shoulders and gently shook him.

"How far can you take your love of solitude and inventions, my fantastic friend! Were you in this tree when you got the foundations of our chalet dug?"

"Yes."

"Oh, Astrobus," Elegant cut in, "we're dying of curiosity. Show us how you did it?"

The dwarf grinned, pointed to the forest and said, "It's there."

"I've got it!" Tobio spun around in a circle. "Remember what Astrobus said yesterday with the fay? He was wondering if there was anything to be learned. Well, Astrobus never stops wondering until he finds an answer. And I've got it."

"Tell us, Tobio."

"Our inventor managed to hire all the sprites, gnomes and pixies of the forest to work for us. Am I right, Astrobus?"

"Oh, it wasn't hard," he answered. "I know they're very curious and very eager to meddle in other people's affairs and since you earned their affection at the same time as the fay's, I used their inclinations. Yesterday, when you were starting to dig, you probably noticed how carefully I was marking off the shape of our building? Afterward, on a high branch of this pine tree I put a piece of bark on which I drew it out and wrote how deep it should be. It was a good idea since we were barely asleep when the merry band started the work, which they carried out exactly according to my instructions. I woke up this morning with the birds. Seeing that my ploy worked, I did it again. If the mountain dwellers really want to, tomorrow night our fortress will be finished."

"Bravo, Astrobus! Your mind, this time, is stronger than our muscles and our guts. So, we'll let you lead the operations."

"I suggest our dwarf friends take a rest and eat after they've finished the foundation. Then all of you can cut down 132 pine trees, very straight and less than twelve inches around, which you can pile up here. In the meantime, I'll mark the trunks where they need to be cut. With a little effort, the work will be finished tonight."

"Great!" Tobio said while Elegant walked to the sectaphore and brought out some mushroom pies carefully wrapped in fresh leaves and a few bottles of flower-flavored dew. There was no need to call the dwarves. Their greedy noses had already announced that a snack was being served. Sitting cross-legged, their eyes twinkling, they unhooked silver goblets from their belts and held them out to Tobio who was beaming because he loved doing this—giving to others fulfilled his generous heart.

Twenty-eight sumptuous pies, all made by Tobio's dwarf chefs, were gobbled up by the hungry workers. When they were done eating, before returning to their work, the dwarves sat in a circle with arms interlocked to form a chain and they started singing in their funny voices their traditional song, "*Heigh Ho, Heigh Ho*". Tobio sang along, terribly off-key, while Elegant's warm tenor rang out and Astrobus beat time by bobbing his big head.

In a short while everyone was back to work. Tobio liked working as a lumberjack. Elegant kept gloves on his hands as he sawed away and Astrobus made his marks with a pine branch that he'd dipped in a red liquid like a paintbrush.

In the tall pines, the gang of zizis and pixies were quivering with excitement and impatience.

When it was time for the nectar, everything was ready. Dwarves and detectives were so tired that they went to bed right after the meal.

Under the twinkling stars, in the enchanted light from the rings of Saturn, the fortress grew. In the morning, at daybreak, the forest spirits along with the elves danced the Will-O'-The-Wisp Waltz on the roof of the chalet while the wise gnomes, not wanting to attract the attention of the wizards to this brown building, sprinkled the north side of it with a liquid that hardened in the air to look like granite.

"Come and admire Hauroc," Astrobus whispered to Tobio as he shook him awake.

"Ho what?" the sleepy-eyed detective asked. "Who are you talking about?"

"Our fortress. You named all my machines so I figured it was my turn to name our home. I've already set up Halthamyamus in the laboratory and the telescope in the tower."

"Are you telling me the chalet is finished?" Tobio jumped up and ran outside.

What he saw filled him with so much excitement and admiration that he started yelling "Hurrah!" Elegant came out with his hair in a mess and the dwarves were in a panic when they ran up.

The fortress' side facing the rising sun was warm brown, pierced by big windows. On the ground floor was a wide gallery sheltered from the rain by vast eaves built over all of it. Behind, embedded in a tall, treacherous rock that seemed to be its only support, the tower sparkled with its upper part made of crystal.

"Come on, everyone together!" Tobio shouted.

"Long live the pixies, gnomes and sprites! Thank you, thank you!"

"U.U.U.U.U." the echo rippled through the sleep of the helpful little creatures.

The visit of the chalet started with Astrobus as guide while Tobio kept jabbing and poking him happily.

Starting from the huge, brightly lit laboratory to the north was the tower whose bottom was big enough to park the sectaphore, Hup! Hup! and Phylomena. To the south was a spacious sitting room. After that came the dining room with a terrace and separated from the kitchen by a short hallway.

In the middle of the laboratory Halthamyamus stood grimacing but not yet turned on.

The first floor held cozy bedrooms and a big room extending out under the roof.

"This will be my invention room," Astrobus said shyly. "When I get my ideas, I'm obsessed with writing every one of them down on pieces of bark. It makes quite a mess."

"Do whatever you want," Elegant replied. "Anyway, it's nice of you to think of sparing us the sloppy sight."

Tobio had climbed the spiral stairs up to the tower. He called out, "A horse rider! He's coming here! Look, it's certainly a messenger from the King. I bet he's got a mission for us. Oh, but I'd really like to furnish our home."

"And me, I'd like to build a system of defense," Astrobus sighed.

Elegant said nothing, but blushed.

"But it might be serious," Tobio said. "In any case, we can let Elegant take care of the flowerbeds. If the Dream Fay wants to help him, we're sure to have something spectacular. As for us, Astrobus, invent away at your leisure. I've always dreamed of a house with hidden doors, trap floors, windows that open by themselves, walls that listen and warning bells... See what you can do! In the meantime I'll go see what the rider wants. If I can't take care of it myself, I'll ask for your help. Ah, there he is now. Why, it's the sorcerer Callas!"

"Glad to see you again," the sorcerer said, dismounting from his magnificent white horse. "The King sends his greetings along with a message for you, Tobio."

After thanking the elegant messenger Tobio cracked the royal seal and opened the letter. "It's exactly as I thought:

"I'm sorry for disturbing you, my esteemed detectives, while you're probably busy building your chalet, but it's about the health of one of my dearest friends, the sorcerer Nivios. The poor man can't eat or sleep and no longer enjoys this wonderful gift we call life. He claims a monster is haunting him relentlessly. Please, go help him as soon as possible. Then come and tell me what you found. My gratitude awaits you.

"Callas, there's time for you to have the welcome with us, then I'll take my sectaphore and go to see Nivios. While the dwarves are setting the table outside, come see our new home and talk with my two wonderful friends."

CHAPTER VIII
The haunted sorcerer

To get to the sorcerer Nivios Tobio had to go through a region sprinkled with small, blue lakes bordered by yellow flowers. It was no doubt to harmonize the two main colors that the sorcerer had used to build his purple castle trimmed in gold. Once again Tobio was in awe of the refined taste of the inhabitants of this land and its gorgeous nature that bloomed in an eternal spring.

He wondered, "Is it possible to feel unhappy here?"

But that was the feeling he got from Nivios when he saw him lying on a bed of moss in his garden with his eyes closed and his mouth frowning.

"Good day," Tobio greeted him with his contagious smile.

Two gentle, brown eyes, very tired, stared at him for a moment, then the sorcerer held out his hand to the newcomer.

"Hi, detective, did the King send you here to hunt down my ghost?"

"He did."

"That's kind of him. I'm afraid, however, that you're wasting your time because to make it disappear, you'll have to destroy me since it's one with me."

"Do you really believe that ghosts are real?"

"Do I believe? Ha! Do you think I'm crazy? MY ghost? Look, it's right there behind me. When I lie down, it lies down. When I sit, it sits. I had to get rid of all the mirrors to stop seeing it all the time. But I can still feel it. Do you see it?"

"No, not really…"

"That's probably because you have Earthling eyes. It doesn't matter, let's visit my domain. What do you want to see first, the house, the garden, the swimming pool?"

"A swimming pool! I completely forgot about how fun they are."

"I don't understand."

"It's true, I have to explain. My friends and I are building a chalet on Dream Mountain. Up there I saw no ponds or lakes but plenty of streams that can provide water for a pool we can swim in. Oh, good idea! If you'd like, let's go see your pool."

"Gladly. Follow me. There's everything you'll need if you want to go swimming."

The sorcerer led the way down a small path through the pine forest. On each side the ground was covered with a carpet of pink heather. Tobio felt good breathing in the pungent but healthy scent of the evergreens.

"You know," he said, "your domain is one of the most beautiful I've seen."

"Really? I'm bored with it. Like with everything else."

"Boredom is a word that's not in my vocabulary. There's so much to see and learn in nature. There's so much one can do and help with among people. And if you lose interest in all that, you can always try to create something new."

"Bah, what for?"

Tobio forgot to answer because what he saw was absolutely breathtaking. In the middle of a crater formed by low, rolling hills, stretched a lake so blue and clear that he could see the bottom carpeted with vibrant plants. All kinds of weirdly shaped, brightly colored fish were frolicking in the water.

"Is this marvel what you call your swimming pool?"

"Yes, detective. In that pavilion made of pink marble you'll find a swimsuit and a bottle of scented oil."

"Thank you very much, but I don't need the oil. Are you coming in with me?"

"No, I'll just sit here and watch you."

"But there's nothing like a good swim to chase away boredom. Fresh water, moving around, it'll get your blood flowing and you'll be on cloud nine."

"Dragging my ghost into water! No, really. Although, if it could drown… that would be funny, to drown a ghost."

"Don't think about it. If you forget about it, it'll forget about you."

"Go and talk to my fish about it. I'll stay here with my enemy."

The sorcerer didn't even have time to get comfortable before Tobio showed up, well toned and tanned. He ran to a white marble statue overlooking its reflection in the lake. It represented a pretty nymph sitting casually on the back of a winged chimera. Tobio jumped onto the chimera, then climbed onto the shoulders of the nymph. Splash! He dove into the blue water. Under a rain of silvery droplets he became a dweller of the deep. The fish fled at first, frantically wagging their transparent fins to contemplate the newcomer from a distance.

"Come on," a rascally one told his young friends, "let's go tease this four-legged critter. His back ones are so sensitive that if we touch their tips it'll make him jump."

Before the rambunctious fish had finished talking, all the others went and wiggled their tails against the swimmer's feet. Tobio knew they were playing with him. He swung around and caught a few of the scamps and, just to give them a little scare, threw them up in the air. How surprised he was to see that instead of swimming away to safety, the frisky fish mobbed him. Unfortunately, he didn't understand their language, otherwise he would've heard them shouting:

"Again! Again!"

And he would've been caught good!

But the water was dusted with gold as the sun disappeared and on the horizon, in a silver halo, one, two, three… the four moons of Jupiter rose.[4]

Tobio and Nivios sat in the castle's big dining room that was decorated with fragrant plants. Delightful little birds graced the nectar, served by pink dwarves, with their blissful songs. After the meal, the sorcerer went to the window that looked out over the flowery garden and offered a comfortable chair to his guest before sitting across from him.

Saturn's rings had such a strange glimmer this evening,[5] the scent of flowers was so soothing and Tobio was so deeply moved that he started daydreaming. But he suddenly realized he wasn't saying anything, so he looked away from the spectacle and turned to his companion to excuse himself. He could hardly hold back a scream.

There, behind the sorcerer who was dozing off, stood the ghost. It was a tall shadow in the shape of a man but all deformed and completely gray. Once he got over the

---

[4] The four largest moons of Jupiter, Io, Europa, Ganymede, and Callisto, were discovered in 1610 by Galileo Galilei. However, dozens of far smaller Jovian moons were detected, beginning in 1892.

[5] Surprisingly, this is scientifically correct. At opposition, Saturn from Jupiter would look just like Saturn from Earth at 2X. But when Jupiter and Saturn make a right angle with the Sun at the 90-degree corner, people on Jupiter could see Saturn and its ring system side-lit in a way that's impossible from Earth.

shock, Tobio grabbed the knife in his belt and sliced wildly at the dreary phantom.

"Ha, ha, ha!" the ghost chuckled. "Another blockhead who confuses matter with spirit! Ha, ha! Trying to cut the air!"

"Air or no air, you're going to die, pal," Tobio growled through his clenched jaws.

"You want to bet?"

"Yes," Tobio answered, "on one condition—you tell me your name."

"It's easy to remember, young man, it's BOREDOM."

"Of course! Why didn't I think of that before? Well, it's you and me, Boredom."

"Oh!" the sorcerer shook himself. "I must've fallen asleep. I'm afraid I'm not much fun to be around."

"Don't worry, I like being left alone," said Tobio. "That way, I can dream and think as I want. I've just found a way to destroy your ghost."

"So now you believe in it?"

"Yes, I just saw it. It's only here that monsters like that can thrive. They couldn't live on Earth. So, let's go to the King of the Fays and ask him to lend us his magic chariot to go to my little planet."

"You'd go through all that trouble for me? Well, It'd be rude of me to refuse."

"Bravo! While you get ready, I'll tell my friends we're leaving so they won't be worried about me being gone so long. See you later."

The region of the Alps with its steep, white peaks, blue glaciers, flowery pastureland and raging rivers is certainly one of the best places to chase away boredom, Tobio thought as he climbed into the royal chariot. Then he shared his desire out loud: "Off to the beautiful Swiss Alps!"

And they landed in the middle of a herd of cows whose bells were jangling joyfully in the mountain air. It was twilight and all the Alps were bedecked in pink charm. In the distance, the low, gentle sound of a horn reverberated and the whole mountain answered like a gigantic organ.

"What a wonderful place the Earth is," the sorcerer said, "and it smells so nice."

Tobio responded with a smile. He knew that the wondrous nature of his country would make any nasty ghost vanish. Nothing could resist this beauty.

After spending the night in a cozy bed, lulled by the sound of the river, the two travelers, now become friends, drank goat's milk for breakfast with some bread and fresh butter, then they got on their way.

For one whole month Tobio took his new friend from the Alps to the prairies, from the prairies to the Jura Mountains, taking all the different kinds of transportation: trains, cars, boats and planes. Nivios was delighted and found again his zest for life. At least that was what Tobio thought but he wasn't surprised when, one night as the tired sorcerer was dozing off, he saw the grimacing ghost behind its victim.

"Vanish, you foul ghost! There's no place for you on Earth!"

"Vanish! No sooner said than done! But Nivios' heart has to reject me and in order to reject me, he'll have to fill it with a feeling so grand and so powerful that there'll be no room for me."

Crestfallen, Tobio turned away so he didn't have to look at the sneering eyes of the awful creature. He was soon so lost in thought that he forgot all about it.

"I've got it!" he cried out.

"What is it?" Nivios asked in a sleepy voice.

"Oh, my difficult friend, I see that you're no longer interested in nature. I'll get you to be in awe of the art of man now. Tomorrow we'll go to a magnificent opera. You'll hear the most beautiful voices and the most exquisite music. Then I'll take you to the museums where you can see wonderful paintings and sculptures."

"Gladly."

After another month of seeing and listening to the best of what the artistic genius of man had created, Nivios yawned again in an armchair and ironic Boredom cast its gray shadow over him.

"This morning," Tobio uttered impatiently, "we're going to walk. I can't just sit here. I need to move around to find my balance. Let's go visit the famous cave we heard about that on that steep mountain."

"If you want."

"If I want! That goes without saying! I just wonder if you want to, for once," Tobio was frustrated.

It was a warm day and at the foot of the mountain the two tourists stopped at a fountain to quench their thirst. Nearby, in the middle of a prairie, a white farmhouse whose windows were decorated with geraniums and whose garden was full of colorful phlox, looked like it was smiling under its red roof in the bright sun. Barefooted children, tanned like little ripe apricots, were playing under a tree. Two brown cows with moist muzzles and vacant eyes had stopped grazing to look at the passers-by.

All of a sudden, Tobio jumped, "Hey, sorcerer, come and help. See that woman there laboring with her scythe? Isn't it sad that her arms are so thin without a shadow of a bicep? A scout could never just walk on by."

The young woman, who was as pretty as her children, smiled gratefully when she gave the heavy tool to the eager young man.

Her gentle voice said, "You see, I'm alone with the children who are still too small to help me."

"We'll take care of it, isn't that right, Nivios? Then we'll bring in your wheat. No need to think about paying us, we have enough money to share with you. Let us do it."

"Yes, let us do it," the sorcerer repeated softly.

Three days later Nivios was happier than a king. He stood bare-chested, his skin browned by the sun, with callouses on his hands, when he told Tobio that he had found happiness.

"Hard work, fresh air, a good rest with a delightful woman, watching over happy, healthy children, it's marvelous! Nothing like it exists on Jupiter."

Tobio just smiled. Had he finally beat the ghost?

However, on Sunday, while he was setting off for the cave along with Dany, Nivios' favorite child, he saw that he hadn't won yet. On the steep, narrow path, Dany was in the lead, babbling away, then came the sorcerer dragging the starved, shriveled ghost behind him. Tobio was about to pass by him so he wouldn't have to look at it when he heard a scream. Dany had slipped and fallen over the cliff.

Instantly Tobio sent a prayer to Amighty God who answered right away. A tree branch had caught Dany by the seat of his pants. Tobio had to hold back Nivios who wanted to jump after the boy.

"Look, friend, don't ever lose your head. God is always here, so there's nothing to fear. Now lie down on the ground and wrap your legs around this tree. Now you hold onto my legs while I'm bending over the cliff to grab Dany."

"No way, Tobio. It's me who'll pull him up. Grab my ankles and try not to let go. If I fall, make sure you save the kid."

With his heart filled with the most sublime love, the sorcerer risked his life to save another. And the rejected ghost Boredom vanished into thin air.

That evening, as Dany fell asleep under the thankful gaze of his mother, Tobio told the sorcerer, "It's over, Nivios, you're cured. With the ghost destroyed we can go back to Jupiter tomorrow."

"You can, Tobio. Me, I'm staying here where I have a woman to make happy, children to raise and a lot of work to do. I've found happiness here."

CHAPTER IX
A funny story

"And you're sure that Nivios will stay on Earth?" the King of the Fays asked Tobio for the tenth time during the report of his expedition.

"Yes, Majesty. As incredible as it sounds, your friend found happiness on my little planet."

"I feel like I'm not wise yet, detective. I was thinking that there was good in the Universe only on Jupiter. It's true that I only hear about Earth and I've never been there. But I'm not sure that the moons and stars that we see in the infinite sky are inhabited."

"I am sure of it, Majesty. Why would God create an infinity of worlds to put inhabitants on only two of them? If a little star like the Earth is inhabited, the big ones surely are as well."

"Which we'll never know."

"Who knows, Sire. Astrobus is working on creating a machine that will allow us to travel in space and visit other worlds."

"Many before him have had the same dream and failed."

"But if Astrobus succeeds! Oh, Majesty, just think of the marvelous voyages and incredible adventures awaiting us!"

"There, there, my enthusiastic detective, don't get carried away. Go and take a look at what your inventor created while you were gone."

As the sectaphore sped off with its eager pilot behind the wheel, the king went back smiling to his friends to tell them about his meeting with the interesting Earthling.

At the foot of Dream Mountain, Tobio decided to surprise his friends. So, in order not to be seen, he went into the forest, took one of the dwarf paths and reached the summit where he thought he saw two shadows sneaking behind a rock. Tobio was intrigued. Who were they and why were they hiding?

Determined to clear up the mystery, he pretended to go on his way but suddenly turned off the path and parked his sectaphore in the bushes. He got out, dropped to the ground and crawled silently toward the rock. At that moment someone came running up, didn't see him and tripped over him.

"Sarrapatan!" a hoarse voice swore. "What is this?"

"Me," Tobio answered.

A small, squarish man, stoutly built, completely nude, with green skin and red eyes pounced on him and tried to teat his hair out. One good punch on the jaw threw him back against a tree.

"Sarrapatan! What's the meaning of this?"

"It means that if you're not polite to me I'll demolish you," Tobio replied calmly.

"Sarrapatan! What kind of race are you? Where do you come from?"

"From Earth."

"Earth! You're making fun of me. Where is this place supposed to be?"

"Somewhere in the sky. It's a small world."

"What a story! And you just fell off it like this?"

"Yes."

"Can you spit fire?"

"What a question! Have you ever seen someone do that?"

"Fantasimias! What an oaf! Watch."

148

And the little man opened his mouth, sucked in and then spit out long tongues of fire.

"Marvelous!" Tobio said, congratulating him. "And what do you use it for?"

"Of course, you don't know. We're the Guardians of Fire of Jupiter. You see these two red circles on my belly? I'm the chief. 12,670,490 complete men, 2000 trunks and heads, 800 heads are my subjects."

"Why 2000 trunks and heads, 800 heads?"

"That's exactly what bothers me. When we reach 1000 years-old, each of us has to be carried away on the wings of the Golden Dragon to the Land of Eternal Rest. That's how it's always been. But ten years ago the system was broken. The Dragon leaves us either our head or our trunk and our head and takes only our limbs. It's frightful and all my people are upset. What we used to consider the last, fantastic voyage has become an object of fear."

"If you'd like, I'll try to help you. Do you live here?"

"Fantasimias! What a question! In the bowels of Jupiter, near the sacred fire, that's where my kingdom is, silly."

"So, what are you doing here?"

"Do you know the Wizard King?"

"Hmm."

"I was thinking no. Well, he's a powerful monarch. All the people of the planet tremble before him, except for three men who are his bitter enemies. They live on this mountain in a wood house. I have to destroy them and their house tonight and Ramines X will help me fight the fate that's fallen on my people."

"Ha, ha, ha. And you believe this? And how do you plan to keep your promise?"

"We'll sneak up to the house while they're sleeping and spit fire until everything is burned to ashes. There are 5000 of us."

"Well now, that's interesting," Tobio muttered, rubbing his chin where he proudly felt a little stubble. "What's your name, chief?"

"I'm the great grandson of Fantasimias, the grandson of Super-Fantasimias and the son of Ultra-Super-Fantasimias, so I'm Hyper-Ultra-Super-Fantasimias."

"A splendiferous name! Mine is much simpler: I'm Tobio."

"Tobio… Wait, isn't that the name of the terrible enemy of Ramines X?"

"Believe me, chief, Ramines X has only one enemy and it's his Hatred. He martyrs the humble, crushes the weak, wants to make violence and cruelty rule this planet. There are only three of us, young and full of love for all who suffer and committed to vanquishing evil. Come with me, chief, and I'll introduce my friends so you can see if they deserve to be burned."

"Sarrapatan! You're really very nice, but I gave my word!"

"Meaning you simply made a deal. Ramines X will help you if you carry out his orders. So, cancel the deal."

"But his help? I need his help. What will my people say?"

"I have an idea. I'll offer to solve your problem and in return, I'll only ask for your friendship."

"Spirit of Fantasimias! Well spoken! I accept."

"Come on then."

In front of Hauroc, surrounded by a carpet of blue gentian, white edelweiss and roses, Elegant and the Dream Fay were sitting in cute, moss-covered armchairs, chatting merrily. They made a delightful couple, she in her gossamer dress of rose petals, he in his handsome suit of sky-blue silk. With their graceful gestures, lilting voices and good looks, they were the model of perfection.

Tobio, always a fan of Beauty, stopped to watch them. His companion, with his mouth agape, seemed to share his admiration.

"Oh, a rare vision!" Tobio said.

Elegant heard him, jumped up and ran over. "What a surprise! A nice surprise! I was just telling my friend about some of our exploits. I'm happy you're back."

"Me too, Elegant. Greetings, Good Fay. Allow me to introduce my new friend, the chief of the guardians of fire, Hyper-Ultra-Super-Fantasimias."

"Yes, that's me," the chief stepped forward. "See, there's no mistaking it, the red circles are here."

"Charming," the fay said.

Meanwhile, Elegant invited the newcomers to sit down and asked the dwarves to bring refreshments.

But the chief was not distracted. He held fast and said, "My friend Tobio offered me your help. Can I have it right away?"

"Certainly, chief," Tobio said. "First let me tell your story, then we'll find a solution to your problem."

During the tale Elegant whispered a few times, "Extraordinary!"

Tobio finally asked him, "What's so extraordinary?"

"I haven't told you yet that during your absence I moved the big book of wisdom that belonged to your mentor Sirius to put it in a safe place in the tower. Out of curiosity I thumbed through it and I remember that on page 4196, I saw something about this."

"Let's go have a look."

"Yes, let's go look," the chief repeated.

On the second floor of the tower was a small room furnished with a couch, a bookshelf and a large table on which the book lay.

Tobio opened it to the page indicated by Elegant and cried out, "Bravo for your memory! It's right here that my dear mentor deals with the problem. Let's see what he says when he writes about the Guardians of Fire of Jupiter: They aren't doing their work, becoming lazier and lazier every day and the planet is slowly getting colder. The Dragon will end up getting angry and refuse to take them to the Land of Eternal Rest, which they will not deserve."

"Sarrapatan!" the chief shouted. "Stop! I understand. The sorcerer is right. Like every being on the planet, we have a mission to fulfill. Ours is for each of us to work four hours a day feeding the central fire. My father kept strict control. Instead of doing like he did, I just tell my subjects when I mount the throne every ten years that I don't want to play policeman and I trust them to do their duty.

"So, they took advantage of my leniency and now they're being punished. I'll run down and tell my people what I've found and get my kingdom back in shape. Thank you, good friends, and think of me if you ever need anything. Here's my address: Fire Mountain, Central Crater. I'll pass by Ramines X to tell him I don't need his help and he can forget about mine. See you later, I hope."

"See you later, chief. Let me…" Tobio yelled after him, but the chief was already gone. Then he laughed, "Too bad he didn't have business cards. It would be something else to see:

Hyper-Ultra-Super-Fantasimias
Chief of the Guardians of Fire Jupiter
Fire Mountain
Central Crater

"What do you think? Astrobus? Hey, Where's Astrobus?"

"That's right, I forgot about him. He's in the invention room. Now that I think about it, it's got to be ten days since he went in there."

"And you're not worried? Come on, as fast as we can. I hope nothing's happened to him."

CHAPTER X
The great adventure

What Tobio saw through the keyhole of the invention room was a relief. Astrobus was sleeping peacefully against a fantastic pile of bark, all covered in numbers and sketches.

"Did he talk to you about his projects?" Tobio asked Elegant as he came up to join him.

"Sure, he went on and on, always his big idea, his extraordinary machine, his interplanetary voyages."

"Do you think he ate anything during this time?"

"Yes. He told me that during his invention cycles he eats nothing but dried fruit and water. He'll have some in there with him."

"I don't see anything. Go and get some tasty pies along with three bottles of nectar. We're going to celebrate my return. If I can't get him to wake up, I'll break down the door."

Bang bang bang! Tobio's fists hammered.

"Huh? What's this? Where's my Tobiophyllox?" the dwarf groaned.

"Ha, ha, ha, that's my partner, dreaming of me scientifically! I'm here, Astrobus!"

He was awake now and came over to open the door. "Oh, Tobio, what luck! I have big news for you."

"Tell me what it is."

"I just did it."

"Did what?"

"The Tobiophyllox!"

"What are you talking about?"

"The machine, Tobio, the spectacular, fabulous, intersidereal machine!"

"Why did you call it that?"

"Oh, I like the name because it reminds me of the person I love the most and the thing I've spent all my energy and intelligence working on."

"To think that there's so much tenderness hiding under those learned lumps," Tobio smiled. "So, now that I know its name, I'd love to see the machine itself."

"I still have to build it. But the design is finished."

"Are you using solar energy?"

"Of course. The energy from all the suns in the regions we'll pass through. But what's important is that I've discovered a force that makes all the bodies in the Universe attracted to each other. It's a fluid I call Phyllox."

"And how is this Phyllox useful to you?"

"What a question! What happens when you throw something up in the air?"

"It falls back down to the ground. But I don't see…"

"You can throw anything, as far up as you can, it always falls back down. Take your sectaphore thousands of feet up and the engine will stop working but you won't be shot into space, you'll come back to the ground. It's the fault of Phyllox that gets its power from the whole huge planet and pulls all bodies back. It's the same on Earth and no doubt on other stars."[6]

"Nevertheless, I came here without even knowing that Phyllox exists."

"You used the wings of a dream, Tobio. It isn't a body but a big, mental stream that comes and goes

---

[6] Isaac Newton's 1687 description of gravity was considered scientific law until Einstein's General Theory of Relativity, published more than two centuries later.

unhindered because it's not matter. Take the King's magic chariot, it's an air bubble built on imagination. But my machine is going to be very real, modern and comfortable. It'll be made of light matter that's incredibly strong."

"Where will you get it from?"

"I've already made almost enough."

"Here?"

"Yes, behind that wall, look."

It was only then that Tobio noticed that the room was split in two by a partition. In the second part there were milky white, almost transparent slabs piled up. On the ground—gross! There were ugly, purple worms crawling around little gutters full of a sticky paste they were gorging on. After writhing around for a moment, they fell asleep, drooling.

"Astrobus, what are you raising here?"

"Oh, it's nothing new. I had these precious animals in my land. I've been using them for twenty years. It's their drool that gives me my matter. By the end of the week I'll have enough to build the machine."

"I do believe you can do it. Oh, Astrobus, I'm burning with impatience, really excited at the prospect of this incredible voyage. It's decided, we're going."

"Yes! On the Tobiophyllox, we're off to explore the Universe."

"Tobio! Tobio!"

"Oh my, I completely forgot about Elegant," Tobio said. "He's calling us because it's nectar time. Let's go ask him if he wants to go traveling with us."

But as always when he saw good things laid out for him Tobio had to eat before talking. It was only after the sixth slice of tasty pie that he was able to speak.

"Elegant, we have to tell you about our project. Starting today we're going to start building the Tobiophyllox, the famous interplanetary vehicle of Astrobus. In a month it'll be finished. During that time the dwarf chefs are going to make lots of pies like this to fill the pantry…"

"Ho, ho! This time, my friends, you've gone beyond the limits of imagination and optimism! I hope you're not asking me to take you seriously. It's too bad that the Dream Fay already left because she'd see that what I told her about my friends is a real understatement."

"Holy perfumes and silk, Elegant, we're being serious! Are you coming with us?"

"There's nothing to keep me from being away for a day or two since that's how long it'll take us to reach the limit of our atmosphere. Did you forget about air? It's going to get really thin up there."

"Have no fear, I've created a device that'll give us plenty," Astrobus answered.

"So, all that's left for me to do is make a suit for the occasion."

"A few, Elegant, otherwise your mood will sour during the boundless journey…"

As unbelievable as it might seem, with the help of the forest dwellers, the Tobiophyllox was finished at the end of the month. It looked like a giant, white, polished cocoon lying on a huge ski. The two ends were pointed, each a different color: The back was flat black, the front a shiny gray-blue. Both had four "eyes" on each side where powerful telescopes were set up on the inside.

Only one door, located on the hull near the back end, allowed entrance into the Tobiophyllox. And it was magical. The floor was covered with thick, green carpets scattered with flowers so vividly colored that they looked natural. Comfortable, white fur couches lined the walls. The cleverly hidden light perfectly illuminated the walls and rounded ceiling with pearly reflections. The sitting room had a full bookshelf and a drawing table piled with compasses, inks and paper. In one corner Tobio's accordion was waiting for him to sing the songs of his land. There was a bedroom with three beds and three closets, one of which had a mirror for Elegant. The dining room had everything one could ask for and the pantry, cooled by a motor, was chock full of food and drinks.

Elegant finally took it seriously when he found two pink, still empty rooms that he got busy filling up with his chest of crazy suits. When they laughed at him, he said that they were needed for the various planets on which the Tobiophyllox would land.

Tobio stayed inside the two ends where he was fascinated by the engines, machines and instruments. Astrobus explained what they were for and how to use them.

"I think I've got it," Tobio boasted. "I can even drive this wonderful thing all by myself. The ends are basically just powerful magnets. Whereas the back end repels and breaks the contact with the magnetism of a planet, the front end is attracting. When we get to a new world, we just have to use it to send out rays that attract and the star's fluid will pull us in."

"Exactly," Astrobus was delighted with his student. "But tell me, Tobio, what do you think this lever and the motor attached to it do?"

"I've tried to figure it out but I can't."

"The ski on the outside will keep us afloat in case we land on water. On land, you just have to pull this lever for the bottom of the ski to open up and expose a series of small wheels that are driven by the motor."

"Do you know that you're a genius, Astrobus?"

"Luckily for my inventions, but unluckily for my lumps. Look, I've got three new ones."

"Don't worry about it. Without them you wouldn't be the little wonder that you are. But I forgot to ask you what you figured on doing with the two pretty rooms that are still empty."

"Hush, it's a secret."

"Oh, Astrobus, please tell me. I love secrets."

"Well, the Dream Fay made such a fuss that I promised to take her along. Of course, we'll say nothing to Elegant before we leave."

"And people say scientists are heartless," Tobio sighed as he casually looked through one of the telescopes. "Hey, Astrobus, the King of the Fays and his court are coming to pay us the promised visit. Don't tell him anything about the vehicle yet. Let's go meet him at Hauroc."

"Good idea. I was so busy building that I forgot to show you the whole set-up of the fortress. Let's go see the king and I'll give you a demonstration."

Soon after the King arrived at the chalet, he told Tobio, "It looks fabulous. Strength and beauty together. See, the door is wooden and very simple. Go figure that I thought it'd be made of iron and impenetrable."

"Don't be fooled by appearances, Majesty," Astrobus said from a balcony. "Try to open it."

Smiling in front of his friends, the monarch grabbed the handle and opened the door. Standing in the doorway was the most frightening, scowling iron monster he had ever seen.

"Try the other door, Majesty," the sorcerers shouted.

No sooner said than done and Halthamyamus growled from the back of the laboratory, "Enterrr... Enterrr..."

The King laughed heartily, "Marvelous! I'm convinced you're well-guarded. Can I come in now, clever scientist?"

A dull thud and the main door opened wide and welcoming.

"Show us more of your wonderful inventions, Astrobus."

"Gladly, Sire. Go into this small room with your friends, close the door softly behind you and whisper to them a secret. However softly you talk, I'll hear."

The King came out after a brief moment, "And what did I say?"

"You told your friends Tobio's favorite saying: Nothing is impossible."

"Unbelievable," the King and his sorcerers exclaimed.

"Oh, there are a lot more interesting things. For example, the basement that goes all the way to the Dream Fay, the magic mirror and in the tower is the telescope that can see into Ramines X' palace."

"If that's true, I'll give a fortune for that instrument."

"Majesty," Tobio broke in, "Hauroc and its mysteries are at your service. You will be perfectly safe while we're gone."

"Gone?"

"Yes, we've decided to make a big trip in the Universe. We're going to see if other worlds are inhabited and by whom. Our interplanetary vehicle is finished. In three days we'll leave from the plain at the foot of our mountain."

The King was so astonished he couldn't answer. He just followed his detectives to see the Tobiophyllox.

When they got back home the King and the sorcerers were still dumbstruck by what they'd seen, but they were excited to tell their friends, who in turn related it to whomever would listen. Soon from the Land of the Fays to that of the Sorcerers, from the Wizards to the Sprites, from the mountains of the Dwarves to the plains of the Giants, everyone knew the astounding news.

On the last night, before saying goodbye to their chalet, the three friends took the Tobiophyllox down to the plain and decided to spend the night on board so they could leave at dawn.

In the morning, when Astrobus woke up very early to make the final preparations for the departure, he wondered if he wasn't dreaming as he took one last look at Hauroc: The entire mountain seemed to be moving. Not a single tree without a dwarf or sorcerer or sprite perched in it. The pastel robes of the fays softened the metallic flashes of the sorcerers' clothes. In the tower, the King's trembling hand was holding the telescope to his eye.

"Hey, Tobio, Elegant and you, pretty fay, come and say goodbye to all of Jupiter. We're leaving!" Astrobus cried out.

While he ran around looking happily and bemusedly at the crowd, while Elegant squeezed the fay's small hands in his own, the Tobiophyllox rose up, rose up and disappeared.

Only the King, through his telescope, could see the little point of light vanish into space… then nothing.

"There they go, the Great Adventure begins," he said in a voice trembling with emotion, envy and admiration.

HÉLÈNE GISIGER

TOBIO

LA GRANDE AVENTURE

A NEUCHATEL
AUX ÉDITIONS DE LA BACONNIÈRE

TOBIO, HIS GREAT ADVENTURE

CHAPTER I
The Departure

While the King of the Fays back on Jupiter was try-ing to watch the small dot of the Tobiophyllox in space, the passengers of the interplanetary ship, all excited by the adventure, were keeping busy.

Astrobus was in the back among the complicated in-struments that only he knew how to work. He was going to load the end facing Jupiter with Phyllox fluid that re-pelled the magnetic pull of the planet. Theoretically he had confidence in his invention, but would it turn out per-fectly in practice? When he was about to start, a slight doubt was gnawing at his heart, turning his cheeks bright red. His chubby little hands were pulling feverishly on the levers while his eyes kept glancing at the control panel where the success or failure of the departure was being displayed.

Meanwhile, Tobio, always the optimist, was whis-tling in front of the oxygen machine and then adjusting the telescopes that served as windows. The planet was al-ready disappearing behind the cottony blue clouds sur-rounding them and the Tobiophyllox was soon entering the eternal night of interplanetary space in search of new worlds.

The Dream Fay had slipped away into the kitchen to let out the dwarves and pixies she had hidden in the cupboard before leaving and who would become the staff of the Tobiophyllox. She had barely opened the door when ten pixies, twittering excitedly, popped out and settled on a shelf or pot or wherever while three dwarves, dressed all in white, respectfully surrounded a round little person who looked dignified and serious. It was none other than the head chef of the King of the Fays who had begged the monarch to let him go with the travelers, not out of love of adventure but for the glory of his craft and for Tobio. Cooking for such as him was a pleasure! When he had invented the Grand Jupiter Pudding, who had come to congratulate him? Tobio, the famous detective. And who was teary-eyed with delight when he had tasted his Steak Cream? Tobio again. The fays and sorcerers ate what was given to them without showing the least satisfaction. But Tobio always gave grateful smiles and kind compliments to the creator of such exquisite things. They'd even become friends since Tobio had nicknamed him Tomaton because his face looked like a ripe tomato. Likewise, because of the detective's ravenous sweet tooth for caramel, the chef called him Caramus.

Tomaton, behind the round body and double chin, had a sharp mind and lively spirit. Banging his slotted spoon three times against a pot to get everyone's attention, he started giving orders in a voice so deep it sounded like it was coming out of a cave.

"You, pixies, there, sharpen the knives and peel this fruit! You, dwarves, grind these hazelnuts and almonds into a smooth paste. We're going to prepare a Full Moon Soufflé for the occasion."

"Can I help you?" the Dream Fay asked shyly before this imposing character.

"I'm sorry but I like to be the only master on board. And no women under my command! With all due respect to you."

"And to you," the fay replied kindly, holding back her laugh until she was out in the hallway.

That was when the thing happened. Astrobus had been sweating bullets while watching the needles on the control panel and was becoming really worried. They looked like they'd gone mad, spinning around one way then the other, twitching and fluttering, pointing north and south, hot and cold, a high and low altitude all at the same time.

"But, but…" he stuttered as he wiped his forehead, "I…"

He had no time to voice his confusion because the ship had just lurched free of the magnetic pull of the planet. The jolt was violent. Thrown against the fluid tank, with his lumps all black and swollen, Astrobus gawked at the instruments. The needles were back to their normal selves and oh, goodness, the Tobiophyllox was flying smoothly on its way.

"But, but…" he stuttered some more as his hands trembled with joy. Then he jumped up and ran off to announce the good news to his friends.

He found Tobio stuck headfirst in the telescope tube, kicking wildly to free himself.

The Dream Fay, by one of those happy accidents that always rescue lovers, had just started cuddling in the arms of Elegant.

As for Tomaton, after bouncing three times from the pot to the wall, he was furiously yanking the pixies out of the precious soufflé base, which was in danger of tasting like…

When he felt his ankles being pulled, Tobio stopped fidgeting and squeezed his limbs as close as possible against his body to reduce his volume so he could slip out of his prison more easily.

"Ouch!" he cried when he fell on the ground. "What happened, Astrobus? Heavens, have you seen your head? Is your machine still safe and sound?"

"It's fine now, Tobio. We just pulled away from Jupiter's attraction, but I'll admit that I was scared it wouldn't work until the last minute."

"How could you ever doubt your invention, Astrobus? I…"

But Tobio didn't finish his sentence. He stood gaping at Elegant who had just shown up in one of the most eccentric suits he'd ever seen.

Tobio managed to stammer, "My word, we're embarking on the most fantastic voyage in a one-of-a-kind vehicle and you're thinking about your clothes?"

"Excuse me," the sorcerer corrected, "but realizing that the experiment we're conducting is, in fact, very serious, I figured I'd get into character."

"Character? What character?" Tobio guffawed.

"Interplanetary voyager. Look, practical pants tight at the knees and leaving my legs free, a soft jacket and aviation shoes."

"Is that really how you describe your get-up?" Tobio couldn't help laughing. "I don't see pants but a jumble of orange ruffles. On your purple jacket those gold stars are blinding. And the crescent moons you're wearing instead of shoes leave me speechless. I won't even mention the rings covering your fingers or the perfume that's suffocating everyone around you. Ha, ha, what a funny friend I've got."

"I could the say the same about you," Elegant laughed back. "Look at your figure, no sense of beauty, of line! Misshapen pockets bulging with sweets, I bet, sleeves rolled up unevenly and those scruffy pants without a crease."

While the two friends were teasing each other, Astrobus, who didn't understand the jokes and hated conflict, was getting worried. Hopping from one foot to the other, trying to find a way to make peace, he reached out as if to separate the combatants and stuttered, "But, but, but…"

The Dream Fay at the end of the hallway put an end to the squabble.

Astrobus cried out, "See what happens when you judge people by their appearance. Would you believe that Tobio and Elegant, taken together, are like brothers? The same courage, the same loyalty, the same generosity."

"And would you believe," Tobio added laughing and poking Astrobus in the ribs, "that this dwarf with such funny black lumps on his head is the most stylish friend here?"

With a sly smile and knowing what effect her words would have, the Dream Fay simply said, "Dinner is served."

The effect was like magic. Tobio, recognizing that he was starving, spun around and shouted with joy how lucky he was to have a female presence on board who thought of the important problems and solved them.

In the dining room, in front of the splendidly decorated table, Elegant looked lovingly at the Dream Fay while Tobio ogled the menu written on small, pink cards:

Milky Way Soup.
Cloud Crêpes.
Neptune Roast.

Full Moon Soufflé.
Nectar and Caramel.

Astrobus had barely sat himself down when one, two, then three dwarves entered ceremoniously carrying a golden, fragrant soup in sky-blue bowls.

When it came time for the light and fluffy Cloud Crêpes, Tobio smiled with satisfaction. With the Neptune Roast he was exuberant. And when he tasted the Full Moon Soufflé he cried out, "Why, it's like Tomaton made it himself! It's the most delicious thing I've ever eaten. There's a peculiar aftertaste to it. I'll be earthbound again if I can guess what it is! Just for the flavor it's a grand success."

But when he saw the caramel cut into thick pieces as he liked, Tobio couldn't resist running into the kitchen to see the artist able to fashion such exquisite delights. Standing before his oven, glistening with red hands on his hips, hat tipped back, Tomaton was yelling at the pixies:

"And watch out, boys, if my soufflé doesn't taste good. If you had an ounce of honor, you'd show the greatest respect to the base! No bump or jiggle can justify…"

"Tomaton, old man," Tobio burst in, "I would've sworn you had cooked the meal yourself. And the soufflé! It's your masterpiece! I challenge any chef or connoisseur to guess the seasoning. A unique flavor. Tell me, what'd you put in it?"

Tomaton glared at the pixies who were stepping forward proudly and answered humbly that it was a secret he'd found recently and then he slyly changed the subject, wondering if his friend Caramus had tasted his favorite dish yet?

"No, Tomaton," Tobio replied, "I came to get you to have the nectar with us."

While they were heading back to the dining room together the pixies in the kitchen made a big ruckus jumping off a butter churn into a big bowl of flour.

"Delighted to see you again," the Dream Fay said with her playful smile when Tomaton entered. She handed him a glass of nectar and added, "I can see that you're going to be a most precious friend to us during this voyage."

This last word startled Astrobus. "But, but, I think we're kind of forgetting that we're on a voyage. In fact, where are we going? It's time to figure it out."

"Right you are! Let's make our itinerary," Tobio said. "Dream Fay, where would you like to go?"

"Oh, me, I'd love to go to Venus."

"Naturally," Elegant smiled, "but my father used to say there's no planet as marvelous as Neptune."

"I'm not much of a dreamer," Tobio said, "but I believe that I could become one in the Rings of Saturn. What do you have to say, Astrobus?"

"Uh, since I've met you, Tobio, I have to admit that the Earth is more fascinating to me than any other world. But maybe Tomaton has an idea?"

"Me? Well, you know, it's not the planets that interest me but what they produce. Now, it seems to me that the Sun would have fruits like nowhere else."

"So many different ideas!" Tobio said. "How can we please everyone?"

The Dream Fay suggested, "I have an idea. Let's draw lots to see which of us gets to be the first to make his wish come true."

"Hurrah! Bravo!" they all shouted.

"So, I'll wrap four different color ribbons in identical packages. Whoever picks the blue one wins since that's the color of our King. There, pick one. I'll be the last. Who won?"

"Don't be upset," Tobio said timidly, "but it's me." Then he got excited and exclaimed, "All hands on deck, explorers! Man the telescopes and machines! En route for Saturn!"

CHAPTER II
The black star

Astrobus and Tobio went to the machines. As for Tomaton, no project whatsoever could distract him from his
passion—cooking. So, he went back to the kitchen. The
pixies, who didn't hear him come in, were caught in the
flour and the dwarves in the jam. Their chief had to bellow
in his cavernous voice to get things back in order.

Elegant and the Dream Fay would have felt very
awkward if they'd been asked to name where in space
they were. They were much more preoccupied with their
joy of being together than with the legions of stars that
filled the celestial universe.

"Hey Astrobus," Tobio called out as he passed by the
phyllox gas tank, "I hope you emptied the tips of the
fluid."

"Of course I did. There'll be plenty of time to fill
them with the attracting fluid when we're in sight of Saturn. But I wonder where it is? Do you see it?"

"No, but I think we can only see the Sun and we're
getting closer really fast. I'm afraid that if we don't fill
the tip with the repelling fluid right away, we won't be
able to avoid to be burned to a crisp. Let's go!"

As soon as it was done, the Tobiophyllox seemed to
slow down, hover for a moment, then slowly go back-
wards. With the danger avoided, they went back to the
telescopes to study the Sun.

The glorious star seemed to fill the sky. From its
sphere erupted gigantic explosions of atomic flames,
glowing, life-bearing gases that sped through the universe. Blinded by the rain of light that fell thickly over the

Tobiophyllox, the voyagers could see nothing of the Star-King. Like every scientist consumed by curiosity, Astrobus tried better and stronger binoculars and telescopes, but all in vain. Without Tobio holding firm to his idea of going to Saturn, he would have gone into the Sun itself.

A frightful jolt shook them out of their reveries and knocked them to the ground. Tobio got up first, with a big bump on his forehead. He started grumbling while rubbing his bruised legs.

"Stupid ship! Lousy machine! This isn't fun and games, it's murder! Is there any machine more vicious than this one?"

"But, but, but..." Astrobus stammered, struggling to his feet and wincing in pain, "it's our fault. We filled one tip and then forgot about it. There must be another celestial body in our path and the law of attraction is doing its job, that's all. I hope nobody's hurt!"

"Not hurt," Tobio said, "unless hearing a volcano in my head and limping counts. And you? You're having a hard time getting up. Like I said, it's murder."

"Go to my room, Tobio, and on the top of the dresser, you'll find a blue flask. Pour just one drop on your forehead and another on your leg. The pain will stop immediately. Find out about the others and take care of them in the same way before coming back to me."

Tobio, who was usually in perfect health, didn't like pain very much so he obeyed his friend without hesitation.

Like Astrobus had said, the liquid was magic. It barely touched his skin when the horde of devils rummaging through his head with pitchforks vanished and his leg was back to its strong, agile self as if by magic. Then he went in search of Elegant and the Dream Fay in the place he'd last seen them.

The jolt had flung them into the telescope and since it was a big one they both got stuck in it headfirst. Tobio had a lot of trouble pulling them out. When he was preparing to treat their injuries, they all broke out laughing.

"What a charming incident!" Elegant exclaimed.

"What a delightful voyage!" the Dream Fay added.

With his hand on the flask's cork, Tobio asked, "What, you're not hurt?"

"Hurt?" the fay replied. "What an awful word. What do you think, my elegant friend?"

Elegant answered with a beaming smile, then put his hand on Tobio's arm and declared, "Keep your potion, we've found a stronger one. Nothing bad, no harm can come to us from now on."

"Really?" Tobio said. "Well, suit yourself. I'll go to the kitchen to see how they are."

Tomaton's plumpness and the nimbleness of the dwarves and pixies had saved them from disaster but nothing could keep the flour, cream and flavorful liqueurs in their containers. There was the most frightful mess on the floor with all the dishes and utensils, pots and pans, fruits and vegetables.

In the middle of the mayhem Tomaton was screaming, "This isn't a job, it's tyranny, it's anarchy! And this machine is an epidemic!"

But Tobio had stopped listening. He realized that the Tobiophyllox wasn't moving. He left Tomaton to his ranting and dashed back to Astrobus who was still sitting down but scribbling figures and formulas on a board. On seeing Tobio he cried out:

"It's exactly what I thought. Mathematically, we must have crashed into a celestial body that hides near Earth, but that the Earthlings don't know anything about, and it is so dark that I've nicknamed it the 'Black Star.' I wonder what's on it... It might be worth exploring it since we're here."

"All right, Astrobus, but let me sprinkle some of this on you first. You can't walk in the state you're in."

As soon as it was applied, the magic potion worked its magic again. As full of life as ever the dwarf jumped up, then grabbed Tobio's arm and dragged him to the door.

"Halt! Remember that we're not on Jupiter. A little patience, darn it. The first thing we have to do is get our bearings."

"Well, I can help you with that," the Dream Fay walked up to them smiling. "We're on top of a rocky peak."

Tobio confirmed, "That's what threw you into the telescope. And I can see a deep valley down below. No trace of animals or humans. This should make for a fun descent. I'll prepare the ropes. Tell Elegant that I've got a pair of durable pants for him. And when we're outside, don't open the door for anyone. Our home here is impregnable from the outside, don't forget."

A short time later, his eyes sparkling with impatience, a rope hung over his shoulder and with soft rubber boots on feet, Tobio was back with Elegant dressed in green leather decorated with red buttons. Astrobus looked his part in a brown doublet and shoes of the same color.

While waiting for the bags that the Dream Fay had brought from the kitchen to be filled with provisions, the explorers toasted a glass of nectar to the success of their mission.

At last, everything was ready. After a bunch of advice for the fay and for the chef and his helpers, who were huddling around them, the three friends opened the first door, closed it carefully, then Tobio opened the second

174

door even more carefully. He stuck his head out and breathed.

"Hurrah!" he shouted. "Breathable air! It's all good, let's go."

He started by tying the rope tightly to rock and he descended, followed by Elegant and Astrobus. If they looked up they would've seen in the windows the pixies jumping up and down excitedly and Tomaton shaking his head with his arms crossed over his belly. The Dream Fay was staring tenderly at the tip of the green hat, the only thing visible of her beloved friend.

"Curious vegetation," Tobio remarked at the bottom of the rock. "Look at these gray flowers and this black moss. I don't like the colors. For once, your clothes are a joy to look at, Elegant."

He replied, "Ugh, those trees! The trunks and branches are furry and deathly pale. Not pretty at all."

"An insect!" Astrobus hollered. "I've got it!"

In his fingers, the dwarf was holding a bug as fat as a June bug, slimy, squishy and cold, which managed to wiggle free and take refuge in a hole.

"The animals here are lovely as the plants," Elegant sighed.

That was when they saw the Grand Stairway and the Pyramid at the top of them.

Tobio's mouth dropped open in wonder. He looked at his companions. They, too, saw it and the expression on their faces testified to their utter astonishment.

In front of them rose a stairway into the air without any support, almost vertical and very high. At the top was a platform on which was a kind of grand mausoleum in the shape of a pyramid.

"That's what I call architecture!" Tobio said in awe.

"Hmm, more interesting to see than to use," Elegant remarked.

"I'll get lumps on my back before I figure out how it's held up. Let's be cautious, maybe it's just an illusion," the dwarf declared.

"Caution, illusion, doesn't matter to me. I've got to go up there and get a look at that monument. Are you with me, Elegant, or have your muscles suddenly rusted? But you, Astrobus, you can stay here and keep watch. If anything happens, whistle."

Elegant would've rather burned at the stake than be considered a coward—he was right behind Tobio. From the tenth step they started to feel so uncertain that they stopped talking. Soon, however, the sorcerer, in order to lift the weight of anxiety that was pressing on his chest, tried to joke:

"And I thought I brought clothes for every occasion! We'll need a robe and helmet covered in springs to land safely if we fall!"

"Don't think about the drop, keep looking up," Tobio grumbled as he got down on his belly, unashamedly, and started crawling.

He was going up, that was what counted. The final steps were really hard and when the two courageous climbers reached the platform, they were turning green and feeling nauseous.

"I believe," Tobio took off his backpack and sat down, "that it's time to check our provisions. I'm dying of thirst!"

Elegant did the same. Rifling around they found a gourd. Tobio put his to his lips and rejoiced in the strong, heady liquid that poured down his throat.

"Oh, wonderful Tomaton," he muttered with all his attention focused on the fresh and tasty liquid. "I've never drunk anything like it. What do you think it is?"

"Nothing but the Grand Elixir," the sorcerer responded. "They drink it nowhere but at the King of the Fays' and only on special occasions. It has great revitalizing power, don't you think?"

"I do indeed," Tobio exclaimed. "Now I'm as hungry as a wolf. Let's have a picnic."

Astrobus still had his backpack on and was sweating anxiously down below, standing on tiptoe and straining his neck to see what was happening with his friends whose backs were against the pyramid. For the moment he didn't even think of enjoying the treasures of Tomaton or the landscape around him.

All of a sudden a whistle broke the silence. Elegant calmly put down the pie he was cutting while Tobio jumped up and leaned over to see what danger was threatening them.

Astrobus was alone but coming out of the furry forest was a parade of shadows. They passed by the dwarf whose teeth were chattering in fear and silently climbed the stairway, step by step. Tobio wasn't able to utter a word before the first shape got to the mausoleum and was swallowed by the door, which had opened up from the inside without a sound.

The two explorers were standing firmly with their legs spread apart, their muscles tensed, watching and waiting, ready to defend themselves with force if necessary. But not one of the shades veered off its path or seemed to even notice them. As the last one disappeared into the monument Tobio grabbed his friend's arm and dragged him in. Before Elegant realized what was happening the door closed behind them.

"Look, those things are in a mist," Tobio whispered.

Elegant looked up and his mouth dropped open in amazement. All the shades were being stretched out, elongated, frayed and frazzled to become one with the swirling clouds like water in a river, then through the ceiling to vanish into a dark tunnel.

In time, they were alone and Tobio let out a deep sigh of relief, "Strange things!"

"Indeed," Elegant agreed, looking around for door. "Strange thing also to come into such a place without thinking first. But since you were smart enough to get us in here, I guess you're smart enough to figure out how to leave."

"Oh, right, the door's gone," Tobio admitted after realizing what happened. "Well, too bad, we'll look for it later. Right now let's see what's here."

"It's going to be a short visit. One room, smooth, black walls, a ceiling the same now that the clouds have disappeared, that's all, I think."

"The Grand Elixir messed with your eyes and mind," Tobio smiled. "What about the tunnel up there and this big movable button that's vibrating under my foot?"

He hadn't finished talking when a warm gust blew by and a voice as deep as a cello spoke, "Why have you come here? Poor creatures, leave now!"

Elegant was about to answer that he wanted nothing more than to get out of this place if they could just find the door, but Tobio heard a hint of a plea in the voice and tried to use the opportunity to satisfy his curiosity.

"All right, we'll leave, but first tell us where we are and what those shades were."

He got no answer. But he felt himself swept up and carried away on a strong, warm current up to two black holes. When he stopped moving he felt a pressure on the back of his head forcing him to stare into the holes while a voice murmured, "Look!"

He saw the courtyard of a middle school, the one he went to when he was young. It was the end of the day; the students were laughing and bumping their backpacks into one another. Suddenly one of them lunged at a poor, shabbily dressed, scrawny kid and started pummeling him with his fists and insults. The others ran up and shouted, "Come on, we're gonna thrash Chenod!"

It'd been many years since Tobio had lived through this scene and he still felt ashamed, deep down inside. When it had happened, he wasn't yet very physically strong or morally brave, otherwise he never would've let it happen.

He even remembered how he'd run away because he couldn't stand the sight. When he got home he'd told his mother everything and she got mad and had yelled at him, "What? And you let them all gang up against one? You should've called them cowards for hitting a kid because he's poor and small and timid. Who cares if they turned their anger against you. You would've fought for justice. Sure, you would've come back with a few bruises, but proud and happy! In the future, don't let things like happen without reacting. God will always give you the strength you need to defend the weak."

Now Tobio was not only reliving his behavior but he could feel the suffering of the poor kid during that unfair fight. He followed him back to his poor home. Nobody was waiting for him. Nobody comforted him. The mother was at the factory and they'd put the father in an asylum for drunks.

Tobio saw the kid slumped in a chair, his head on the kitchen table, crying his eyes out and he felt such a heartache that tears welled up in his eyes too. That was when the strong gust of wind came and carried him away to the bottom of the stairs where his two friends welcomed him with joy and bewilderment.

"I insist on getting the key to this new mode of transport," the sorcerer said. "To think I believed you were kidnapped, lost, and here you come triumphantly riding the wind like the King of Air himself."

"Don't laugh," Tobio replied gravely. "Let's get out of here. This star isn't a place for us, and it never will if we keep struggling to be good and to love our neighbors. But wait, how did you get down here, Elegant?"

"Oh, it's very simple. After you were taken away and had disappeared into that tunnel, someone I couldn't see pushed me to the door that opened on the platform. It closed behind me and since I didn't see you coming back, I ran down here to Astrobus to figure out how to save you. But here you are and the problem is solved."

"We're not going to abandon our exploration!" the dwarf contested. "I haven't figured out yet how these stairs are being held up."

"Don't get upset, Astrobus, if I beg you to go back. It's not right for us to come and disturb the shades on this star as they brood over their faults and repent them. Let's go back to our ship. A good climb will make us feel better."

"But I'm hungry," Astrobus complained. "I don't see how you two can go running and climbing all over the place without even needing to drink something."

"Sorry," Tobio sighed, "our gourd's empty of the famous Elixir and we've already drunk what was in our backpack."

"I should've figure that," Astrobus chuckled. "You could eat in the middle of a fire. Let's sit down and lighten my provisions so I don't have to carry so much."

"Never in my life…" but Tobio didn't finish because Astrobus had snuck up and poured some liquid down his throat.

Soon afterward, the three friends were climbing merrily. When they reached the ship, they were greeted by the smiling fay and the whole band of the Tobiophyllox. It was agreed to get the machine started up again and it wasn't until they were high up in the sky that they told the story of their adventures to the eager audience sitting around them on the red carpet.

CHAPTER III
The uninhabited paradise

Tobio had such a passionate way of telling stories that his listeners lost all notion of time and place. He was describing in vivid adjectives and expressive gestures the wind-force that had carried him into the tunnel and, later, to the bottom of the stairs when another jolt, luckily not so violent this time, struck the ship.

They were all, even Tobio, so caught up in the story that they thought it was an effect of this mysterious power. The first to come to his senses was Astrobus. He grumbled, "We're idiots. We should just go back to Jupiter if we don't know how to travel better than this."

"What's the problem?" Tobio questioned. "Why are you complaining?"

The dwarf barked back, "We've just crashed again. Not surprising since we take nothing seriously and think only of having fun."

"If taking everything seriously means being in a bad mood all the time, then we're not doing it. Let's make the most of whatever happens to us, it'll be so much more interesting. Myself, I've always believed in an invisible pilot. On Earth, we call it God. Let's go see what work He's got in store for us."

The Dream Fay and Elegant, attracted by the landscape they saw through the windows, agreed impatiently. Tomaton, along with the dwarves and pixies, was lugging a huge basket for potential supplies of fruits and vegetables.

The voyagers were barely out of the ship, intoxicated by the pure air and a vision of exceptional beauty, when they shouted out in joy. This new land looked like paradise from its vegetation. Succulent fruits in abundance and the exotic flowers opened their mellifluous cups to big, satiny butterflies all of one color: red, orange, blue or black. The trees were teeming with animals that looked like small monkeys with mischievous miens and meager movements. One of them, to the great amusement of everyone, came and sat on Elegant's shoulder. It froze in admiration, or so it seemed, of his big red buttons. In this peaceful environment the songs diffused by the streams and birds sounded like real hymns of joy.

Tomaton tasted every fruit, smiled, and was already devising the most marvelous recipes for unique beverages, tasty jams, creams and puddings.

The Dream Fay was making friends with the butterflies. They were coming from all corners at the sound of her sweet voice. Probably they thought she was a new kind of flower.

Meanwhile, Tobio, Astrobus and Elegant went off in search of the happy beings who must have peopled the planet. They walked for a long time without finding a trace of habitation. No paths with trampled grass, no cut down trees, no dammed up rivers. Beauty, peace and harmony reigned alone in this place.

All the animals and plants were in perfect shape. The animals were plant and fruit eaters, which delighted Tobio. No carnivores who committed murder every time they wanted to appease their hunger. Colorful beetles glittered like precious stones everywhere. Fat bumblebees with their black and gold stripes buzzed through the air along with honeybees. They could zip through the sunlight without being harassed by flies and mosquitoes. No evil thoughts of humans troubled the atmosphere of the planet. No vicious insect lived here.

Tobio sighed.

Elegant noticed that his friend looked lost in a dream and asked, "What are you thinking about, Tobio?"

"About my mother. Can you imagine that this is exactly the country she dreamed of. She often described it in the stories she told me. It's here she used to fly to in her imagination when her earthly dwelling became too hard. We have to bring her here someday, Astrobus."

Cheered up by this idea, Tobio was suddenly back to his energetic self.

"Let's go back! This resting place is not for us. We have to keep learning and fighting for the good causes."

In the midst of this pleasant nature, they had gone a long way without realizing it and it was only when the last rays of the sun were fading and a dozen moons started glowing in the sky that they got back to where they had started from. And what a nice surprise was waiting for them! The chef had a delicious meal prepared for them on the prairie grass.

"Tomaton," Tobio said, "you're full of bright ideas. Tell your helpers to join us so we can all eat together."

While the band of explorers were sitting in a circle talking and laughing, filling their bellies, all the animals gathered around them, intrigued by these new beings. After the meal, Tobio went to get his accordion in the Tobiophyllox, but it wasn't easy getting through the wall of living creatures. The curious white rabbits and pink squirrels were in the front row, crowded by the clumsy little black bears and the dumbfounded giraffes. Zebras had followed the others there and were having fun nibbling on their tails while a troop of red monkeys were tickling each other on top of a gracious elephant.

As Tobio passed by, he got sniffed and licked. "That's enough!" he yelled at a monkey who decided to perch on his head and start pulling his hair.

When he finally got back to the ship, he dove inside to keep the animals from coming in after him. He quickly grabbed his instrument and hurried back to the camp where he sat off to the side and looking off into the distance started to play the most beautiful tunes from his childhood.

The others listened, laid down and dreamed away. Tobio remembered the pristine peaks of his own small country, its green pastures, its tall pine trees and the merry chimes from the cowbells in the evening when the sounds of nature faded away.

That was when a beautiful planet encircled by colorful rings appeared on the horizon.

Astrobus was the first to see it and stammered, "Sa… Saturn."

The accordion wheezed out a long sigh and folded up its bellows when Tobio dropped it and jumped to his feet.

"My friends, I think that you, just like me, are happy to have landed on this planet, but don't forget that adventures await us. Do you agree that we should be on our way?"

"Yes, yes," they cried out together.

"Psst," Tomaton hissed while making quick gestures with his hands. The dwarves and pixies must have understood this language because they got busy immediately. All leftover food was picked up before the Dream Fay could even offer to help.

Saturn had not yet reached its zenith when the Tobiophyllox was disappearing from the view of all the nice creatures watching its departure in utter astonishment.

CHAPTER IV
The incredible rescue

Astrobus stayed by the machines. With the tip filled with fluid, he headed straight for Saturn. Early in the morning, when the ship stopped abruptly, he nodded suspiciously and went to wake up Tobio.

Being startled awake he asked, "What's wrong? Have we crashed again?"

"Um, it would seem so. I don't understand. There must be a little planetoid in the vicinity of Saturn and with all the brightness from the rings I didn't see it. I would have taken off again without telling you of the incident, but something incomprehensible happened."

"What is it?"

"Well, the truth is that, even though we're right by the first ring, we can't get through. The Tobiophyllox hit the planetoid while it was flying around trying to pass through. Maybe it eould be better to stay here and study the problem before pushing on in vain."

"What you're saying is very intriguing," Tobio said. "Let's wake up the others and have a good breakfast. After that, we'll go and explore this new world."

When he got to the kitchen, Tobio saw that Tomaton already knew what to do because he was busy with his pots and pans, barking orders, tasting this, sipping that, stirring here and there. Elegant showed up dressed in a crazy purple suit perfectly tailored to his strong, supple body. In the dining room the Dream Fay was setting the table and arranging flowers on it.

"Why are you up so early?" Tobio asked.

"Do you think we can sleep through an earthquake?" Elegant laughed. "Jolts like that could shake the wrappings off a mummy."

"Oh," is all Tobio said as Astrobus sneered at him on thinking of the trouble he had waking him up.

With Tobio mealtimes were always long and fun. This morning, however, still half-asleep and with his mind full of questions, he was eager to find out about the place where they'd landed. They saw a grayish glow, not very welcoming, through the windows.

"I think," Tobio said, "that it'd be better if Elegant and I go alone to check it out. I can't explain why, but I don't like this planet."

"I agree with you," Elegant responded. "I'll follow you."

"Here are your provisions," Tomaton announced proudly at the door, "and before leaving, here's a glass of the Grand Elixir."

Tobio said nothing. He reached out for the glass while his brown eyes looked as gentle as ever when they met the chef's. Astrobus, with his usual scientist's foresight, gave them an excellent spyglass. When everything was ready, the two friends left the others to guard the ship and set off.

A pale sun barely dissipated the heavy fog that spread over the whole land. After a tough march over the swampy ground, they came to a stretch of water on whose shores was a group of round huts made of dried mud. Poor, bent, pale and timid creatures were working around the huts. The strongest were putting the mud from the beach into big buckets which they carried back and emptied into molds lined up on the ground. The weaker ones were smoothing them out with a board then leaving them exposed to the Sun. Still others were removing the dried bricks and stacking them up into pyramids.

"There are only women and children here," Tobio observed. "They look miserable! Let's go talk to them."

He said hello in the fay language, which he figured was understood throughout the universe. "What are you doing?"

The three children he addressed lowered their eyes and answered shyly, "Bricks for the King's castle."

"Well, take a break and come have some pie with us," Tobio suggested kindly.

"We can't stop to eat until midday," the one who looked the oldest said, "or else our fathers won't have enough bricks to finish before the third sun and they'll all get a hand cut off as punishment."

"I'd like to see someone try that while I'm around!" Tobio shouted.

"Mercy, mercy, let our children work, or else they'll lose their lives," the women moaned.

"All right, but tell me where the men are," Tobio said.

"On the other side of the lake, behind the hill, five days and nights in slavery for the Lords. For one day and night, they can come back to work on their own homes and in their fields; then, they go back with the bricks we made during their absence."

"I'd like to meet these tyrants," Tobio snarled at this friend.

"We'll kill them," Elegant was already flexing his muscles.

The two friends walked along the lake for a long time without anything but ugly, warty toads and a kind of yellowish reptile with the body of a snake and the head of a lizard that spit black bile at them. When they got to the foot of the hill, they decided to take a quick break to eat and rest.

"Seeing those poor devils took away my appetite," Tobio admitted while nibbling on his pie.

"Me too," Elegant replied curtly.

Impatient to act, they got back on their way and soon reached the top of the hill from where they could see the homes of the Lords, big and complicated buildings of brick that covered a lot of ground surrounded by greenery.

The women and children of the masters looked happy and well fed as they strolled and played or sat on the grass in their gardens tended by slaves. Farther off, a group of men were building a huge castle. Fifteen tall, smooth towers were already pointing their spires to the skies. The workers were erecting the sixteenth.

"Let's go see the worksite," Tobio said. "We ought to find the men we're looking for."

Staying unseen, they got to the place exactly when a shrill siren went off. The men stopped working and trudged, bent double, silent, to a balcony on which twenty or so lords stood tall and strong, dressed in silver.

"Only one of them is wearing gold," Elegant whispered in Tobio's ear. "That's got to be the king."

Tobio scrutinized the person who stood out not only because of his magnificent clothes but also because of his strong jaw, his prominent belly and his arrogant eyes. The little finger of his right hand bent under the weight of an enormous black diamond. He stepped forward, leaned over the crowd of workers and spoke to them in short phrases that cracked like a whip.

"There are still ten towers missing from my castle! It doesn't look like you care! Woe onto you, lazy slaves! If the last tower isn't standing before the first rain, your children will be butchered. To start, I'm taking away your break time. Go get the bricks and come back right away. Anyone not back before the end of the moon will be food for my dragons."

Not a sound arose from the terrorized workers. The sad troop went trudging back to their village.

"Let's pounce on those savage beasts right now!" Elegant said in a voice trembling with anger.

"Shh, I've got an idea to punish these brutes better than just beating them up. But we have to act quickly. Come on, I'll explain on the way."

Being fit and healthy the two friends easily got ahead of the slaves despite a detour. Tobio was excited and skipping instead of walking.

Elegant demanded, "Tell me what you've cooked up. It's frustrating seeing someone all excited without knowing why."

Tobio grabbed his arm and started poking him in the chest. "One of a kind! Marvelous! Fabulous! Do you know what we're going to do, Elegant? Leave that gang of lazy, cruel lords to get by on their own. If they want ten more towers for their palace, let them build it! If they want more castles, they'd better get to work! And if they want to eat, let them farm their land! Let them make their own clothes to wear! Since they don't know how to appreciate and respect the noblest thing in the world, namely work, let them learn how to do it."

"Are you going to organize a slave revolt?"

"Thank you, but no! I've got no desire for disorder. I have a better idea. I want to take the slaves away."

"Take them away? I hope you don't plan on putting them all in the Tobiophyllox. I will be impossible to travel!"

"You don't get it. We're just going to take these poor people to the uninhabited paradise we just left. They'll learn to live and be happy there."

Elegant, usually so calm and composed, twirled around gleefully. "What an incredible rescue! The Dream Fay is going to be so happy. She'll be an eager aide. And what a good lesson for those noble lords! It'll be fun to come back in a few years to see what's become of them, don't you think?"

"For the moment, I'm just thinking about our plan. Maybe you should warn our friends and bring the ship over. In the meantime, I'll talk to these people."

Elegant had been gone for a little while when the slaves reached the village. The women and children ran up to hug them tearfully. Sitting on the tallest hut, Tobio put two fingers in his mouth and whistled in imitation of the alarm. All the terrified heads turned to look up at him.

"Good people," Tobio told them, "I come from the little star that you see tonight next to the first moon. I have visited a few planets and recently discovered an uninhabited paradise. Good grass, beautiful flowers and savory fruits grow on the fertile ground. Birds, butterflies, lightning bugs and peaceful animals roam the land. The sun is gentle and the air pure. Your children will grow up healthy and happy in this blissful country. I saw how disgracefully they treat you here and I want to save you from the tyrants and from this miserable land. Do you want to go?"

Skeptical from so much suffering the men said nothing but the women, with hope already in their hearts, squeezed their children tightly and shouted, "Oh yes! Oh yes! Right away!"

At that very moment, the Tobiophyllox came gliding up. At the sight of this incredible vehicle, the men started fidgeting because they, too, were beginning to believe the miracle was possible.

As soon as the ship stopped, the Dream Fay stepped out, almost glowing with beauty, and while the children gawked at her like an angel coming down from heaven, chubby Tomaton, with the help of the dwarves and Elegant, covered the ground with a pretty blanket and spread out juicy fruits and tasty pies.

The fay was now surrounded by the children. She gave them peaches, but since they'd never seen such things they hesitated to bite into the silky fuzz that tickled their lips. One of them got brave, however, and sunk his teeth into the golden flesh. Juice gushed out and splashed his neighbor. He was so surprised by the freshness and taste that he gobbled it up noisily. The example was contagious. All the other children, even the adults, jumped on the food and ate greedily.

"I feel the teacher waking up in me," Elegant whispered to the Dream Fay. "We're teaching these people how to eat well."

In the meantime, Tobio, always practical, counted the people who could be transported and started making preparations. He had to hurry because night was coming on. The curious children, now full, surrounded the ship and, when the pixies appeared at the windows, they cried out to be let in so they could see up close these fabulous little creatures.

"Perfect," Tobio said. "All of you go in and the mothers will follow."

"We can't abandon our young ones who are still in the service of the Lords," an old woman declared.

"That's a complication I hadn't thought of," Tobio admitted, "but I'll deal with it right after you leave. I can promise you that when the next moon silvers the sky, you will all be reunited in a new land."

The Tobiophyllox was full. The Dream Fay, Tomaton and the dwarves, on Elegant's orders, entered and started organizing the trip.

Tobio approached Astrobus, who was so shy that he had stayed beside his machines and told him, "I'm counting on you to take these people as quickly as possible to their goal. Once there, drop them off with the fay and Elegant who will help them and come back immediately because I want to avoid fighting by surprising the Lords with the sudden, inexplicable disappearance of their slaves."

After one last handshake with his friends and a friendly goodbye to the emigrants, Tobio scrambled down the short ladder that led from the ship to the ground. The Tobiophyllox closed up, seemed to quiver as if its carcass was suddenly coming to life, glided off and then rose up and soon disappeared into the dark sky.

A good while later, all the men were still in the same position, petrified by astonishment, mouths open, watching where the ship had vanished.

"Hey!" Tobio yelled. "If we're going to rescue the ones still in slavery, let's go! We have no time to lose. I suggest that the youngest and the most brightest of you who know the layout of the castles go right now to warn them to come back tonight. You can't get caught. If you do, let them cut off your heads before you say anything about our plan. Losing your life means little if the sacrifice saves so many others."

He hadn't finished talking when a young man, not very tall but sturdy-looking, stepped forward. Tobio stared into his honest, heroic eyes and immediately felt a connection. They shook hands.

"I'm Tobio and I want to be your friend. What's your name?"

"Seggor," the young man answered in a deep, mellow voice.

"Seggor, you have the heart and mind of a leader, I feel it. Choose your partners and take control of the expedition."

When he saw the face of the men glowing with pride, Tobio knew how much they loved and respected Seggor. Everyone wanted to go with him, but he chose only ten men, figuring it more prudent to keep the numbers down, which Tobio approved. Loaded with provisions, they sprinted off into the night.

"And now let's try to get a little sleep," Tobio smiled at the comfy cushion that Tomaton had the foresight to leave him."

It had been less than an hour since he had traveled to the land of dreams when a strange sound woke him up.

"Let's hope Seggor thought about the dragons," someone nearby said.

"They went to their death," another declared.

"And what's going to happen to us," an old man wept.

Figuring that these poor devils were going to start panicking, Tobio had a clever idea. He pretended to be just waking up, stretched slowly and yawned, then he got up and smiled.

"My friends," he looked at his watch, "rejoice because your wives and children have arrived in the uninhabited Paradise and should already be running around merrily on the green pastures. And then the rescuers and rescued will soon be coming back from the castles. In the meantime, what if we prepare one last good prank for the Lords?"

A few voices muttered, "Ehem…"

"After you've left, your masters will be astonished by your absence and will come to punish you. Do you know who will be waiting to greet them in village? Armed men in aggressive poses."

"Ha, ha, ha," a few young men reacted. "We can't believe it."

"Well, we'll see about that," Tobio said. "Let's go, you castle builders, use your mud and each of you build for me a man, strong and scary-looking."

When they finally understood what he meant, they all started working and laughing like children. It was a contest to see who could fashion the scariest one. When the first lights of dawn appeared at the same time as the men and women escaping their servitude, the sight of the village terrified them so badly that they ran away screaming.

"Hey, hey, come back! It's a trick," the sculptors shouted, calling them by their names.

They came back, amazed by the change in their mates. While Tobio explained things to them, a tall old man with a thin face counted the new arrivals.

"They're all here and I think Seggor and his friends will be here shortly."

Indeed, as day chased away night, the expedition returned. Tobio didn't notice it because, up above, in a big cloud, a black spot was moving, growing, getting closer by the second.

"The Tobiophyllox," he sighed with relief.

Presently, the ship landed and Tomaton came out very excited.

"It's done," he told Tobio. "You should've seen it! The kids went wild and the women cried with joy. As for the Dream Fay and Elegant, they took their roles very seriously. They officiated gloriously, convinced that they were born to lead people to happiness."

"Well, now that's something," Tobio sounded surprised.

The rising sun brought them back to the present.

"Come on, get in, quickly!" Tobio told the men.

They all obeyed except for the old man who had tears in his eyes. "I'm sorry, but I can't leave my Seggor behind."

"Seggor! What, isn't he here?"

"He let himself get caught in order to rescue us," a young girl answered sobbing.

Tobio gazed thoughtfully at the ship, then at Astobus and Tomaton next to him. He took the old man's arm and led him gently to the ladder, reassuring him, "Go in peace. I'd never abandon a friend in need. I'll save Seggor and bring him back to you."

"I thought valiant knights only existed in legends," the old man was deeply moved. "You've proved me wrong." And he stepped confidently into the Tobiophyllox.

"I'm staying too," Astrobus stood hands on hips and face set in stone.

"That's all I need!" Tobio pushed him into the ship. "Do you want to ruin our plan? Go get these people to safety and come back to get me."

Thinking of nothing but the ship now, the dwarf slammed the door and ran to his machines.

"He's crazy, completely out of his mind," Tomaton grumbled as he saw his idol staying behind. But he kept calm and, with the Tobiophyllox already shuddering, he opened the door again and threw a big bag outside.

"Good Tomaton," Tobio muttered to himself when he saw the avalanche of creamy caramels, the Full Moon soufflé and the bottle of Elixir spill out of the bag. "Life will never lose its charm with you."

In the morning sun, among the fierce mud warriors, he had his breakfast. As he was sipping the Elixir, he saw something moving on the horizon. He dropped down on his belly and crawled over to the nearest hut. There, behind the rickety wall, with no weapons but his intelligence, bravery and an army of mud men, Tobio was ready to fight the brutes and save his new friend.

CHAPTER V
Tobio the nanny

In the castle kitchen, they were busy in the morning. They had to have the excellent meal ready for when the Lords woke up. Gone soft after years of idleness, they had their breakfast in bed. Behind every door, ready to run at the slightest noise, a servant slept.

Today, Zatron, the earliest riser of the Lords, woke up in a very bad mood. Pale, beady eyes, severe lips, hair sticking in the air, he propped himself up on his elbows and growled the name of his servant. Nothing moved. Raging mad, he grabbed the whip off the headboard and roared. No answer. Huffing and puffing, trying to control his anger, Zatron got up and stomped to the door, which he flung open. In the face of an empty hallway his fury was replaced by stupefaction. If the sun didn't rise or the moon vanished, he could understand it, but that his slave, his thing, would take such liberties, he couldn't even imagine it.

When his brain was working again, he ran downstairs howling curses. In the empty kitchen the ovens were off. Then his heart was filled with dread. What would happen if the slaves revolted? Who would do their work? He was hungry and had no idea how to prepare his breakfast. He was thirsty and would have to filter the water or find out where his servants kept the bottles of fruit juice. It took him a long time just to solve these problems. After that, exhausted from the uncommon labor, he struggled into his clothes, unbrushed and the silver unshined.

From next door, he heard a man yelling and children crying. No trace of servants.

Little by little, the Lords showed up in the streets, badly dressed, waving their arms in anger. They headed for the King's palace. He was in a state of extreme anxiety, pacing back and forth on his balcony, hands behind his back, frowning. The sight of his subjects' alarmed faces calmed him down.

"My friends," he told them, "it seems that we're facing a great conspiracy. We have to act quickly and crack down hard. The guilty parties, with their people as witnesses, will suffer the most atrocious torture. We must snuff out any desire to do this again. Arm yourselves and we'll go surround the village. Don't forget the chains to drag the prisoners back here."

The idea of action and punishment energized them. It didn't take long to organize a troop under the command of the King. While marching, they talked excitedly and ended up coming up with a solution: skewer all the rebels' children and bring the men back to the castle, bound and gagged.

Suddenly, the sharp eyes of the King spied the first huts and the terrifying army in front of them. The monarch exclaimed, "That beats everything. These scoundrels are waiting for us, looking ready to fight and armed to the teeth. But we've got a big advantage over this bunch of buffoons: intelligence. So, let's use it. While we draw up a plan of attack, two of you will go sneaking over there to scout out the secrets of our enemy."

Through his binoculars Tobio had watched this episode and knew from their expressions what was going to happen. He let the spies get close to the mud soldiers. When they discovered what their enemies were made of, they broke out laughing. One of them even dared to enter the empty huts.

He shouted, "Their revolution isn't too dangerous. The wretches are hiding somewhere, no doubt trembling in fear and regretting their revolt. But we can't give in to pity. We'll have to crack down hard on them."

On hearing these cruel words, Tobio couldn't just sit there. When the man approached his hiding place, he jumped out and, before his adversary could react, he punched him in the jaw. The Lord was knocked out and the chains he carried for prisoners were used to tie him up.

"Hey, Zatron, where are you? What are you doing?" a nearby voice called out.

Tobio hurriedly hid his victim in a hut and came back out ready to fight.

The young noble was waiting for him with his glistening blade drawn. The Lord barked, "On your knees, vermin! I'm going to cut off your filthy hands that dared to touch a master!"

Tobio started to bend down, then charged like a ram, headfirst into the belly of his enemy, knocking him to the ground.

"Two down," Tobio murmured before he started whistling while he dragged his new hostage to lie tied up next to the first. Realizing that the two men could wake up and start screaming, he tore his handkerchief in half and gagged them both.

In the meantime, the King was getting worried that his scouts hadn't come back, so he sent three more to look for them, ordering them to report back quickly with any information so that he could launch the attack as soon as possible. But the sun reached its zenith and nobody came back. Tobio had put all his smarts and all his strength to good use and they'd been wrapped up like the first two.

Although the monarch pretended to be brave and never missed an opportunity to exercise his cruelty, he was, deep down, a coward. When his five scouts didn't return, he smelled something fishy. Logically, he couldn't send his troops forward with only a small rear-guard to protect himself, so he puffed himself up and shouted loudly to cover up his worry.

"We could attack the village to free those men who obviously fell into some kind of trap. Or we could go back and come up with some serious plan of attack. I'm leaning toward the second option, but I'll let you choose. Whatever you decide, I'll be your leader."

The bravest were already in Tobio's hands. The others were happy to rally behind the King's proposition. The whole troop retreated fast. The last ones kept looking back, scrutinizing their path, but they saw nothing but the twitching shadows that followed close behind them.

The women were waiting in the big plaza and their voices could be heard far away. Fat, lazy and not very clever, they lived to sleep, eat and get dolled up. Their white hands with long nails painted black couldn't even swaddle a baby. Normally, they got everything they wanted; they were waited on and pampered, and they stayed calm and happy. Today, however, faced with this ordeal, they whined and complained, but didn't once think of doing anything about it.

Only the children seemed to take some pleasure in the situation. Left alone, they raided the pantry and gardens, then ran from one castle to another, having themselves a ball.

The babies in their cozy beds cried from hunger for hours, then fell asleep.

It was with one of them that Tobio managed to enter a room to hide. The baby stared at him with its big brown eyes as it sucked its thumb greedily but not able to get any liquid out of it, the baby whined sadly. Feeling compassionate, Tobio went in search of food. Since there didn't seem to be any milk on this planet, he was satisfied with a silver bowl full of strange, brown fruit. He stuck a spoon in it, got some juice and poured it gently into the hungry mouth.

At the same time, he thought of all the other innocents who would suffer and maybe die because of the slaves' freedom. Sunk in this gloomy meditation, remembering how hard it'd been to do, he lost all notion of time and caution. And that was how the King and his wife found him.

"Who said you could touch this baby?" the monarch yelled.

"My conscience," Tobio answered. "It was hungry so I fed it."

"Your conscience? What's that? If it's an animal, get it out of here. Then I'll keep you as a slave. Get going, start to clean up now."

"Excuse me, I'd like to stay with you, but only to take care of the children. Yours has eaten now, so I'll go see to the others."

"Since when did a slave dare say 'I'd like to'?" the King was turning red with anger. "Bunch of filthy vermin, wretched trash! Just wait and see what I'm going to do to you! I'll pulverize you. I'll exterminate you!"

"And you'll be alone," Tobio replied calmly. "Instead of using your strength to do evil and make martyrs out of your fellow man, you can use it to work. Only then will you become men."

During this time the queen, who, like all the other women of the realm, felt sick at the thought of taking care of children or doing any kind of chore, knew the benefits of owning at least one slave. Afraid of losing him, she put her hand tenderly on the King's arm and cooed:

"You see, friend, how tired all this has made me. Leave him in charge of the children. The big ones can take care of themselves. As for the castles, well, we'll wait for the slaves to come back to clean them. Our supplies and our well-tendered gardens will give us enough to eat. If you follow this sage advice, we women won't be too stressed and you men will have plenty of time to put the kingdom back in order."

This speech put an idea into Tobio's mind that filled his heart with joy. Without giving the King time to respond he said, "Oh, Queen, I swear to watch over your children lovingly and to make real men out of them. Since it's so hard for you to take care of them, I'll relieve you of the burden. Give me two towers being built and send them all to me, the big ones can carry the small ones."

Happy at the thought of solving this problem, the Queen went to the balcony to tell her subjects about the new project that was welcomed readily. Before the nightfall, in the first tower, all the babies were lined up next to one another making the most astounding concert. The second tower was for the older children and Tobio sat in the middle of them telling them how a fantastic ship piloted by a dwarf appeared in the sky one night.

A little girl with big, curious eyes interrupted him, "What did it come to do?"

"It came with a beautiful fay to take you all away to the most marvelous land."

"Oh, I wish it were true," a boy sighed.

At that moment Tobio saw in the window a long cigar appear in the sky and then disappear behind a hill.

He asked, "Would you like the story to be real?"

"Oh, yes, yes!" they all clapped their hands.

"Psst," Tobio whispered like he was telling a secret, "I'm going to get the dwarf and his flying chariot, but you can't make a noise or leave here or else he'll get scared to come. Promise?"

"Yes, yes," they all whispered back with their eyes wide and their fists pressed against their chests in expectation.

"To pass the time," Tobio added, "I'm going to leave you my little companion."

He took off his watch and hung it on the wall.

"See, it has three legs. Look how active the little one is, running around in circles. But it's the biggest one you should pay attention to. It's going to reach this black number here, which means, in watch language, it's eight o'clock. That's when I'll leave. You'll see it move around and when it reaches the six on the bottom you stay very calm and quiet because I'll be behind the door with the dwarf."

Feeling confident about the children, Tobio ran off to meet Astrobus who got worried and was coming to look for him.

"What a relief! You're here!" the dwarf cried out. "But where's the other? These trips are no fun. Luckily this will be the last one."

"I don't think so," Tobio replied shyly. "I haven't found Seggor yet. There was so much to do for the children! Come on, we've got to be very careful getting the ship to the castle. The kids are waiting there."

Tobio didn't hear the dwarf's grumbling or see him shaking his head in disapproval because they were coming to the Tobiophyllox and Tomaton, the picture of cheerfulness, was filling his vision with his chubbiness.

"An exquisite lemonade, a pile of caramels, some pies and brand new dishes are ready," the chef announced.

"Tomaton, I already told you, you're a treasure but I don't have time. Fill my pockets with sweets while I pilot the ship. Luckily the night is very dark because we have to act in secret."

At the controls, his sharp eyes on alert, chewing absentmindedly on the candy that Tomaton was slipping into his mouth, Tobio reached his goal by going around the hill so they wouldn't be seen from the castle.

Standing at the door, he asked nervously, "Are your helpers here, Tomaton?"

"Just the dwarves."

"Good. Have them bring the babies nice and gentle. The trip won't be long so they can be laid side by side on the carpet and then fed. In the meantime, we'll take care of the bigger kids. Come on, I promised to introduce them to the dwarf who's going to take them to wonderland. I'll knock on the door and you go in first. I think it's time."

Indeed, under the careful watch of many pairs of eyes, the big hand had just reached the expected number.

A girl's timid voice said, "What if he's behind the door? Maybe he can see us through the lock?"

Scared, the children held their breath and huddled together.

A knock echoed through the room and almost at the same time a jolly, chubby Tomaton appeared. His belly so round, his cheeks so red, his smile so beaming, how could he not win over the children at first sight?

They all cried out in joy, "Hello, good dwarf!"

"Hello, my little friends. Are you ready?"

"Yes, yes," they shoved one another forward.

"Gently, gently," Tobio advised from the door. "Let's line up in pairs and enter the magic chariot well-behaved."

Fascinated, the small group promptly got lined up and entered. When grumpy Astrobus came to see what was happening, he almost tripped over the wriggling, babbling bundles on the carpet. When he turned back to take refuge in the corridor, he was ambushed by a group of kids who were touching everything and running everywhere. Ah, really, it was unbearable! He couldn't think in all this racket! He would put everything in order and right away! He started to scold them but, being all worked up, his voice came out like the croaky whistle of a cold steam engine train.

Curious about the lumps on his head and his weird language, concluding that he was a strange species of rare dwarf, the children kept prancing around him and tried to drag him with them.

Tomaton, after leaving Tobio behind with the provisions for a dozen meals and a bunch of rope, had closed the door and gone to give the signal to leave. He snickered at the picture of the little passengers and their pilot, then he spun around and went back to the kitchen but returned immediately with a big basket full of caramels.

He said, "My friends, do you like good things? Sit down and open your mouths."

The children obeyed at once. Astrobus was stupefied and learned the value of this method because the wild savages were transformed into little angels.

After the ship had gone, Tobio ate alone, smiling at the thought of the rocket speeding through space full of babies, children and dwarves. Truly, we sometimes see really extraordinary things in life!

CHAPTER VI
In the dragon's lair

Nocturnal searches had always been fruitful for To-bio. Therefore, tonight he decided that before getting some sleep, he'd try to find a few clues to where Seggor was. He quietly closed all the doors and windows of the towers and snuck out.

The neighboring castles were dark. No doubt the Lords and their Princesses were tired out by the day's ordeals and were already asleep. Only one light was on in the last building. Without thinking, more like an insect, he headed straight for the light. As he got closer, a hair-raising noise made him jump. It was like a lion's roar, an elephant's trumpeting, a thunder's roll and a siren's wail all in one. Tobio knew it was the dreadful voice of a dragon.

The monster howled continuously and Tobio, led by the sound, soon spied a column of green flames rising out of small gully. He moved more cautiously now and reached the edge of a huge pit, the home of a gigantic female dragon and her children. The beast was spitting fire out of her five mouths at a crevice in the wall near the edge of her lair.

Fascinated by this rare sight, Tobio didn't think at first of trying to find out what the monster was doing. He stood in awe of the glowing green beast at the bottom of the black abyss. The little ones still had only one head but their mouths were wide open, revealing smoldering red fires. The silver-scaled mother was whirling her forked tongues around, cracking them like whips. When her heads screamed, the horrible stench of sulfur infested the air and Tobio automatically opened his mouth to keep his eardrums from being ruptured.

The animal's fury seemed totally focused on the hole she was bombarding with flaming jets. Tobio finally started wondering what could be inside. He got as close as possible and looked into the wide crack. He saw nothing. On the other hand, he did make a discovery that left him thinking. On the wall was a ragged piece of cloth just like the slaves used to make their clothing.

"But that can't be Seggor," he said aloud even though his inner voice of detective was shouting the opposite.

He stood there for a moment, undecided, then his gut instinct made a decision to find out at any cost what was hiding from the bitter beast. But how? He would have to be impervious to fire. But after thinking about it, he figured that if the dragon was distracted he could do it.

He ran to the other side of the pit and started throwing everything he could find at the dragon. The flames changed direction and targeted him. He kept this up for a while, hoping to draw the monster's anger onto him. But by the time he snuck back to his original position, the dangerous jets were attacking the crevice again.

"But if someone's inside, there's no time to lose," Tobio mumbled to himself. "He must be half-cooked or suffocating by now. What can I do?"

In his life, whenever he got stuck in a mess he couldn't get out of, he always followed the advice of his mother and a solution would appear.

"When you feel lost among unsolvable problems," she'd say, "don't fear. Stop and ask calmly for God to come to help you. Wait for his response confidently. It will come soon enough and everything will be all right."

It was time to do something. Tobio knelt down on the wet ground, looked up at the sky, into the stars, where the marvelous and Almighty God Being was, and he prayed. He hadn't even closed his eyes when an unprompted thought came into his mind, suggesting that he get up and walk around.

Astrobus would've called this a good idea, but Tobio knew that angels manifested like this. So, he obeyed and his steps led him to a big pond.

Water! Fire doesn't like this element! Now he had a weapon available but how to use it? The "good thought" suggested that he dig a channel all the way to the pit. Tobio went immediately in search of a tool. He found it at the back of the garden in a shack—a kind of pick-axe that could, in the soft ground, easily dig a ditch that would get bigger the closer it got to the pit so that it sloped down.

He took care to start digging around three feet away from the pond to keep the water from bothering his work. When everything was done, he went back to deal with the last section. Once the final shovelful of mud was tossed aside, a thin trickle started crawling down the channel, then it filled up to form a stream.

With his heart racing, Tobio ran to the pit where the water would rush in unexpected.

For a dragon who feeds partly on its own fire, this water attack was an intolerable offense. Forgetting the object of her former fury, thinking of the danger to her little ones, the mama dragon confronted the crisis with frantic energy, spitting rivers of flame.

Taking advantage of this distraction, Tobio tied a rope to a rock and threw the end of it into the hole. He grabbed hold of it and shimmied down into the hiding place. His feet hit something soft and moaning. When he turned on his flashlight, he gasped in surprise. Seggor was lying there, his clothes blackened, his hair singed, unconscious.

"Holy sprouts, lucky I brought the Elixir," Tobio muttered. "But first of all, I have to get out of here in a jiffy. Who knows if the monster won't start aiming here again…"

Using a well-known mountain climber's knot, Tobio tied the rope around his friend's waist and climbed up first. Wedging his feet against two big rocks, he started pulling Seggor out of his hole. He had just lifted him over the edge when a long jet of flame shot by them. The dragon had vanquished the water and was back to her original prey. Too late, fortunately.

Tobio grabbed his friend under his arms, dragged him away, then lay him on his back. He lifted his head and poured some of the magic liquid down his throat. The effect was almost immediate.

Seggor opened his dazed eyes and asked in a weak voice, "Where am I?"

It was only after drinking the whole bottle that Seggor could thank his savior and tell him what happened.

"We started with the castle where a lot of slaves were. We just had to explain the situation to one of the gardeners or cooks and they went to tell the other staff who organized the escape, being very careful not to alert the Lords with any too hasty action. Everything was going so well that at dawn most of the people were already waiting at the arranged spot behind the hill.

"Only three girls and the slaves assigned to the dragon were missing. We couldn't get them out of the castle except through the windows, which wasn't easy because they were on the top floor. I decided to go alone to the Dragon's Castle because I didn't trust Jabas, the hunchbacked slave who lived there and was a mean boss to the six workers. I suspected he'd betray our people to the Lords. As cruel as he is ugly, he was also their executioner and torturer. He'd throw the condemned into the monster's pit with demoniacal joy. He never came to the village… we would have stoned him.

"I snuck up to the house and got in through a downstairs window. From there, I went into the kitchen where I happened to meet our six brave men preparing the monster's meal. I told them about the plan and rest assured they didn't have to be told twice.

"We were about to reach the meeting point when I saw a shadow following us sneakily. I got worried and stopped. All our spy had to do was sound the alarm and our plan would've failed. But I felt safer knowing that, on this dark night, he couldn't have known who or how many we were. And behind the hill they were invisible. So, all was not lost.

"I gave orders to my companions to climb to the top, then to run to the meeting point in order to warn the others to hurry back to the village because the first lights of dawn were about to appear. Nobody was to come back or else they'd ruin my plans.

"Only once did I sit down for a moment to let the traitor get close to me. When he was within thirty feet, I got up and ran in the opposite direction. I was careful to avoid the castles. The hunchback, since it was him, had good lungs. He kept up with me the whole time. Soon I reached the last building, turned off to the left and came near the pit where the monsters were making a big fuss. There was nowhere else to go because the swamps lay beyond. What was I to do? I turned around but didn't see the traitor so I came up with a way to get him off my trail. Easy, I just jumped into the hole in the wall of the lair.

"That was exactly what the shrewd guy was waiting for. Grabbing the iron pitchfork he used to feed his pets, he stabbed it into the hole trying to skewer me. But I was on guard! I grabbed the prongs and yanked. And something happened that I wasn't expecting. The hunchback, who was holding fast onto the handle, surprised by my attack, didn't let go but lost his balance and fell into the pit, still holding the pitchfork. And that was how the executioner, who had rejoiced in throwing so many of his own people into the dragon's maw, met his end.

"Now with her appetite worked up, the beast was determined not to let her second meal escape. Every attempt to get out of my prison failed until the fires of hell being spewed by my enemy made me pass out. But then you came! How can I thank you? Do you know that I always wanted to have a friend like you?"

Tobio chuckled, "I've noticed that if you desire something strongly enough, whether on this planet or another, you'll end of getting it."

Then he held out his hand to Seggor and said, "From now on, we're friends for life unto death, right?"

"For life unto death," Seggor repeated solemnly with a firm grip.

"Now let's go back and I'll tell you what happened while you were smoldering in your incinerator."

Tobio walked arm in arm with his companion. The two young friends chatted and laughed at the tricks they played on the merciless tyrant of this star until they got to the village where the rescue ship was waiting for them.

CHAPTER VII
The kingdom of dreams

Astrobus was worrying about what other people Tobio might be rescuing when he saw him and Seggor strolling down the hill. He sighed in relief and ran to the kitchen.

"No need for quantity, quality will do just fine," he smiled to Tomaton.

"What do you mean by that?" the chef was surprised to see the dwarf happy after being so gloomy for so long.

"Tobio's back and only with Seggor. I just saw them. After dropping off the former slave in his new land, we can finally get back to our adventure. And it'll be great because we'll have Tobio all to ourselves!"

"Say, Astrobus, might you be a little jealous?"

"I don't think so. Understand that I can devote myself to my passion for inventing and study thanks to Tobio. He doesn't just encourage me, he helps me, too. With him around new ideas keep coming and nothing seems too hard or impossible. How do you expect me to work surrounded by a bunch of windbags! And what more annoying herd can there be than these kids always touching everything and watching everything you do!"

"Astrobus, don't badmouth the children. They're the best and most tender beings of Creation. Smile at them, love them and you'll see they can offer you a precious gift—their pure souls and their unspoiled hearts. Be careful that your science doesn't make you selfish. And don't forget that Tobio, even though he loves the same things you do, is also very generous when he sees injustice and misfortune. I think, Astrobus, that if you want to stay friends with him, you should try to be more like him."

The dwarf didn't have the time to respond because he was startled by Tobio's voice behind him.

"Ah, there you are!"

He had already climbed the ladder with Seggor and was coming to meet them. They all shook hands warmly as he introduced his new friend.

"And he's as hungry as I am, Tomaton. Of course, we'll all eat together from now on, it'll be funner. Astrobus, I think we should leave right away. Our appetites will be healthier the farther away we are from this awful country."

"Can I change clothes?" Seggor asked shyly because he was embarrassed by his shabby rags under the icy stare of Astrobus.

"Oh, I'm sorry I didn't think of that first. I'm always seeing people with the eyes of the spirit instead of the body because it's always their character I see and not their clothes. And you look wonderful to me. Come on, while Tomaton takes care of the meal and Astrobus takes us a mile away, you can slip into a pair of my pants and a new shirt. They should fit because we're the same size."

In the hallway Seggor flinched in fear and put his hand to his chest.

Tobio smiled, "The first jolt. You'll get used to it in no time. Look we're already hundreds of feet off the ground."

"It's all so unreal," Seggor couldn't tear himself away from the window. "It's like living in a dream."

"Let's hurry up! You can come back down to reality at the table."

Soon after, however, while he was enjoying a delicious soufflé, Seggor, who was used to simpler, coarser food, was still wondering whether he was in a dream.

"Do you always eat like this?" he asked Tomaton who was beaming at the boy gobbling up the dish.

"For a guest like you, always," the chef answered. "Holy pots and pans, you're just like Tobio. You're not one of those turnips who just nibble at things. You've got good, strong taste buds that can appreciate subtle flavors. I swear to all the pies in heaven, it's a pleasure to do my job for people like you!"

"Oh, don't get too excited," Astrobus said. "We'll reach the uninhabited Paradise very soon and since we won't be staying there, the young man here won't be sharing our meals anymore."

"Hey, Astrobus, are you off your rocker or are you cooking up a new invention?" Tobio barked. "Young man here, young man there! Did I save him from the dragon's deadly fire just to have a snack with him? Seggor, do you think you'd be happy using the strength that God gave you and the courage and energy that lies in your heart to just daydream on a pretty planet? When I say 'adventure,' do you feel your pulse racing, do you feel wild ideas dancing a jig in your mind?"

"I do feel great fondness and gratitude to all of you and if you'd accept me as your companion, you'll find in me a devoted friend. Tomaton, I'll eat all your masterpieces with gusto. Tobio, I'll give my life for you and if Astrobus agrees, I'll help him with his inventions."

Such politeness caught Astrobus off guard. He blushed. He wanted a fresh start so he stood up and said, "Come on, Seggor, I'll show you the Tobiophyllox and explain how all the machines work."

Happy with his victory, Seggor followed the dwarf while Tobio and Tomaton smiled smugly.

When he looked through the main telescope, Seggor gasped. He saw a giant ball with a luminous ray crossing over it and wrapping around each side.

Astrobus explained, "That's Saturn, a planet thousands of times bigger than the one you just left. See, a quarter of it is in darkness and another quarter in shadow while half of it is lit by the Sun, shining pink and yellow."

"But how can such a big thing hang in space?" Seggor asked in awe.

"Science will explain that in detail, although not completely. Only the Great Force, God, who governs the universe, knows."

"And the shiny line that splits the planet in two, what is it?"

"It's the rings. From here and at this time of the day, they look like that, but from where I come from we can see them clearly, surrounding the star with circles of different colored light."

"Are there a lot?"

"We see three of them. The outer ring, a beautiful dark purple, looks thin. The middle one is almost too bright to look at, maybe the light of fusion. And I can't describe the exact color of the inner ring. It's like all the colors mixed together then made subtly transparent. See, it's like a dream in color."

"Oh, Astrobus, now I understand why Tobio wants to go to a world like that. But I can see another world farther away to the left."

"That's probably the uninhabited Paradise. Come and I'll show you how to fill the tips with fluid so we can land."

Seggor listened attentively to the dwarf's explanations but was still thinking of the telescope. As they got closer, the tiny star grew bigger until it filled the entire field of vision. Then the ship left interplanetary space to enter the bright atmosphere of Paradise.

Soon, they saw the surface streaked by a big river and its many tributaries. The ship circled around and landed close to the mouth of the river, on the shores of a shimmering lake where the people were getting settled.

The passengers had barely stepped off the ladder when a happy, excited crowd carried them away to their new King.

Tobio looked around in a daze on the shoulders of the man carrying him. Charming brown wooden houses were being built everywhere. Even before the houses were finished there were flower beds in the windows and on the balconies. Young girls, rosy and smiling, wore violets in their hair. All the young people had stopped and turned their honest eyes to watch them. Elders were warming themselves in the sun, sitting on soft chairs made of moss. Children were cheering the great magician who had transported them to this fairy-tale land. Their round cheeks, tanned skin and bright eyes were beaming with joy and health.

Looking at them, Tobio's heart was flooded with emotion and his eyes were filled with tears. Ashamed of his weakness, he hid his face. When he peeked over his elbow to see if anyone had caught him, he was surprised to see Seggor doing the same thing.

He whispered, "Are we turning into fountains?"

He didn't hear the answer because the Dream Fay and Elegant had just come out of palace of flowers to greet them. With bluebells in her blonde hair and a robe decorated with wild flowers, with her radiant smile and angelic eyes, the fay was the very image of Beauty and kindness.

But it was Elegant whom Tobio watched in wonder. Not one multi-colored button, not one lace trimming, not a trace of silk adorned his plain, light linen suit. His face looked virile and his deep voice sounded melodious.

When they were alone in the palace Tobio, with his usual frankness, asked, "What happened to your wardrobe, friend?"

"My dear Tobio, you seem to forget that I am now the King of Paradise. Although regular people can do whatever they like, their leader is not allowed. I have to set an example and practice what I preach. To be happy, you have to live simply. My Queen and I try hard to restrain ourselves. Every one of my subjects have the same clothes as we do and eat the same things. The flowers, the wonderful gifts from God, are our only luxury."

"I see," Tobio said, "that you govern with great wisdom and I congratulate you. If the head of a family or a people is upright and good, peace and happiness will reign. But I can no longer call your land the uninhabited Paradise since it is no now inhabited."

"Well, Tobio, since this kingdom is mostly the result of your doing, we were hoping that you'd agree to be its godfather, or mentor, if you wish, and give it a name."

"Aye! But I don't have the imagination for names. The more I think, the more I add h's and y's to already crazy words. But haven't you noticed, Elegant, that the dreams of your beautiful fay used to send to Earth are made real here? The Dream Fay can be nothing else but the charming queen of Dreamland. So, the name's been found, friends, and I'll offer you a bottle of the famous Elixir with its recipe. It'll be the opportunity, when you give it to your people, to drink a toast to the champion of this star."

"You're talking like you're about to leave," the Dream Fay sounded sad.

"Yes, very shortly. Saturn calls us. But before that, I want to ask you again what you did with the Lords' children."

"I adopted them all," the fay laughed. "Only married for a few days and I'm already the mother of forty happy toddlers. Ten girls are helping me take care of them. They'll be raised with the others and given the same education."

"I'd be interested to know about your schoolwork," Tobio asked.

He had painful memories of laborious grammar, long lists of historical dates, nasty numbers that always tripped him up and loads of names of places, rivers, mountains and what have you that he had to cram into his child's brain.

"Most of our program is about love. I also teach my students joy and purity, then we go on to health. Every child learns, conscientiously, to keep their body healthy. Later, we'll take time to teach them about our champion."

"Oh, don't do that. I'm just a poor Earthling full of faults who struggles with himself all the time to become better and who tries to devote his life to helping others. But I'm sorry I can't take classes with you."

"My classes are always open to you," the fay laughed again. "I give them every morning in the flower field right after the sunbeams have feasted on the dew."

"The offer is tempting, but I really do have to go. Let me hug you both."

And so they did. Tobio was no friend of gushing emotions, so he gave the signal to leave, which took a little while since the dwarves had let the children invade the ship. While Tomaton stuffed them with sweets, Astrobus was showing them all the interesting machines.

Tobio was just starting to worry about Seggor not showing up when he saw him coming with his father.

The old man, with his eyes gleaming, held out his hands to Tobio.

"Seggor told me what you did for him. Thank you from the bottom of my heart. I'm so happy that he found a true friend and that you'll give him the chance to experience a great and wonderful adventure with you. Until you return, my thoughts will follow you everywhere."

"Thank you, Sir, a train of good thoughts is never a burden but always a great support. We'll be back, I promise, but maybe not for a long time."

Seggor hugged his father and the two friends climbed the ladder, closed the door of the ship and stood at the windows to wave goodbye to all the people gathered round. The women were crying while the men, the young ones especially, were envious of the marvelous ship going off to resume its journey through the universe.

At the telescopes Tomaton and Astrobus, when they saw the children clapping and sending kisses, were so touched that they couldn't get the machines working properly so that the Tobiophyllox, instead of making one of its grand departures, bucked three or four times before launching itself clumsily into space.

"Hmm, hmm, the fluttering of a sensitive heart!" the new King pronounced in a hoarse voice.

CHAPTER VIII
The mauve ring

"I was thinking," Tobio said suddenly while the ship, with its tips full of fluid, was soaring toward Saturn, "have you figured out why you couldn't get through the first ring of the planet, Astrobus?"

Sitting in his comfortable armchair, the dwarf answered, "No, the mystery remains. Maybe we'll solve it this time."

Tobio's face relaxed. He dropped the conversation, let his head fall back on the soft chair, closed his eyes and didn't move.

Believing he was asleep, Seggor, too, felt calm. But he jumped when Astrobus, out of the blue, rushed out of the room and came back almost immediately with a strange object that he put on the knees of the sleeper.

He implored, "Hey, Tobio, what if you play something for us?"

"What an excellent idea," Tobio sat up.

He slip the strap of the accordion around his shoulder, bit his lower lip, then started running his agile fingers over the keys. From the first sound, Seggor was deeply moved and held his breath unconsciously. Shivers ran down his spine and tears welled up in his eyes. He had never heard or felt anything like it.

Tobio seemed absent, with a distant gaze. Tomaton admired him and Astrobus tapped his thigh in rhythm. Knowing Tobio, the dwarf knew that he was suffering from homesickness at the moment. It happened once in a while, but being able to express it through the accordion comforted him.

The music went on for a long time. Finally, Tobio stopped playing, looked surprised at his companions and then smiled.

Seggor, still overwhelmed, begged, "More!"

"Since you love music so much, how'd you like it if I teach you to play some songs?"

"Oh, Tobio, I think I'd be the happiest person in the world if I could play as well as you some day. It's the gate of heaven that you've opened for me."

"For sure, music can give a lot of joy. Me, I like it for what it conjures up."

"I don't understand. Explain that to me," Seggor said.

"Well, I'll play you a tune quietly and at the same time tell you what it makes me see. Listen. Here I am high up in the Jura mountains. The thin air I breath is full of invigorating scents, the warm and vibrant smell of tall pine trees, the subtle odor of thyme, the perfume of hawthorn, the sweet aroma of pink clovers. In the spring the pastures are dotted with blue gentians, then the delicate campanula come, those silky bells of fairy tales.

"In the shelter of the trees ants are building their cities, fat bumblebees with yellow bellies are on the go, a woodpecker at work is making a mysterious rat-a-tat echo through the forest. Down below the plain stretches between rolling, wooded hills, the quaint villages lie peacefully, one after another, and the lake whose clear water reflects the sky is shimmering.

"Soon, with my companions, we light a fire and cook potatoes and a sausage. Then we set up our tents near a grove of hazel trees, all the while talking and laughing. At twilight, we ponder the valley that night is already covering with its dark wing. We feel wonderfully free and happy up on our mountains. And when the first star twinkles in the sky, only the tinkling bells of grazing cows disturbs the silence."

"It's true, Tobio, that these songs are just as good as words to describe the beauty and serenity of the landscape. I'd love to see it!"

Tobio was about to respond when the whole room suddenly turned to the color mauve. Astrobus ran to the machines, Seggor and Tobio to the telescopes. The purple ribbon of the first ring stretched out in front of them. Neither gas nor water nor matter, it seemed to be made of all three elements at the same time. Its color was so warm, so vibrant that it didn't just enter through their eyes but through every pore in their body all the way to their souls, which it filled with joy.

Tobio was enchanted. His voice trembled when he said, "If you told me that this incomparable, celestial carpet led to the throne of the Creator Himself, I'd easily believe you."

He hadn't finished talking when the ship slipped gently into the mauve expanse. And something extraordinary happened. The bodies of Tobio and Seggor became transparent. The two friends saw their immortal souls and felt incredible joy. They were so beautiful and perfect!

Tobio tried to speak but his voice made no sound.

Nevertheless, Seggor understood him because he answered in the same way, and Tobio, in turn, understood him perfectly.

They lost the notion of time until the Tobiophyllox, obviously having crossed through the first ring, hit a huge, black wall beyond which was the second ring that was so bright it hurt their eyes to look at it.

Faced with this obstacle, Tobio reacted. He ran to Astrobus and wasn't too surprised to see that he, too, was transparent as he filled the tip with fluid to bang against the wall that seemed harder than diamond and darker than the darkest black he'd ever seen in his life. But nothing changed.

Tobio did the same thing but to no avail. He was about to do it again when a head appeared on the black surface. It was an old man with a very long, white beard. His voice, which boomed like thunder, exploded so suddenly that Tobio stumbled backward.

"What are you doing?"

"We want to reach Saturn," Tobio replied bravely.

"In this state? What an idea! Because you are bathing in the spirit of Saturn, it looks like you've gotten rid of your bodies, but it's only an illusion. They're still there. With them, you'll never make the Great Passage that leads to the last ring."

"Oh, Mighty Sprite, perhaps you'd agree to help us?"

"Impossible. It's not in my power to upset that which separates the material world from the spirit world. I still don't understand how you managed to get this far. Tell me, what exceptional act did you do to open the ring of wisdom for you?"

"He saved all my people from misery and slavery," Seggor said. "From a world of hell, he lead them to paradise."

"Oh, oh," the old man said. "No one I know has ever done the like. Well, you've been rewarded since you've reached the higher spheres of wisdom."

Carried away by curiosity, saddened to be so near his goal without being able to reach it, Tobio pressed on, "I'd be so happy if you let us get a peak, just for a moment, at the other side of the wall, O Great Sprite."

"Very well, boy, but then, you'll have to die."

"Die!" Tobio exclaimed. "Oh, I have no desire to die and my friends don't want to either, I'm sure."

"No, not at all," they cried out.

"Do you hear that, Sprite?"

But the old man had disappeared.

Tobio looked once more at beautiful and inaccessible Saturn with its halo of magical rings and without asking the others he put the ship in reverse.

The Tobiophyllox, slowly at first, then faster and faster, recrossed the mauve expanse and was dumped back into the vast universe.

CHAPTER IX
Return to Jupiter

"I'm so sorry we couldn't get to Saturn like you wanted, Tobio," Astrobus sighed.

"But it's better for you, Astrobus. The Dream Fay and Elegant have no say anymore, just you and your wishes."

"Earth! Would you be so kind as to grant me this favor?"

"It's not a favor, Astrobus, since it's been agreed. But I suggest we make a short stopover on Jupiter before going to my home planet. We have so many stories to tell our friend about the fays, the sorcerers and the giants that he'd love to hear. What do you think, Seggor?"

"I don't want to interfere with your projects but, of course, a visit to Jupiter would be thrilling."

"So, it's decided," Tobio and Astrobus said at the same time and they headed for the machines.

Tomaton, ran happily to his kitchen that was soon full of feverish activity. He had to prepare for the King of the Fays the tasty treats made of the fruits and juices gathered in Dreamland.

Seggor didn't move from the telescopes.

As for the dwarf and his friend, sitting at the machines, they were in danger of growing the long beards of philosophers.

"It's strange," Tobio shook his head, "I thought I was over traveling across the universe. Having a house to oneself, a family, friends, animals around, that's what brings true happiness."

"And me, I dreamed of living quietly in my laboratory," Astrobus said.

"Seeing the land we love all the time, breathing its fresh air, what a great feeling!"

It was in this state of mind that the interplanetary travelers got excited to see the blue mists of Jupiter.

A few moments later, in the garden of the King of the Fays, a small, pink dwarf started shrieking while pointing at the sky. When the King was alerted, he left his precious telescope and announced the return of the Tobiophyllox.

The news spread so fast that when the ship was clearly visible all the people of the Land of the Fays were already surrounding the royal palace to welcome the travelers.

The grand banquet hall was opened and the high table in the middle was decorated specially.

"Get back, get back, make room!" the sorcerers cried out to the mob of curious dwarves who were invading the lawn.

Lurching through the air at low altitude with a black cape floating behind it, the chubby Hup! Hup! arrived, driven by Ramines X. The Wizard King landed right before the Tobiophyllox and went to take his place next to the King of the Fays.

Silence fell over everyone as the interplanetary ship landed like a beautiful bird. The door opened and Tobio, tall and mature, with a serious look on his face, got out with his friend Seggor. Behind them came Tomaton, flushed with pride, and Astrobus, so bashful that he didn't know what to do with his hands.

"I hope you didn't lose the Dream Fay and Elegant?" the King said as he hugged Tobio.

"No, Majesty, they're wisely supervising Dream-land. I'll tell you all about it. Allow me to introduce my very dear friend, Seggor."

As the monarch was kindly greeting the young man, Tobio bowed to Ramines X with a surprised look that turned to astonishment when the Wizard King linked arms and led him to the table.

The charming, pretty fays went around with pitchers full of nectar and the sorcerers raised their cups to drink a toast to the health of the travelers. Bustling and babbling, the dwarves climbed up on whatever they could to see the hero of the moment.

All of a sudden, a bell rang and the Queen Mother entered, tiny and pink with her silver hair that was almost a thousand years-old. She sat on the throne of honor and invited Tobio to sit next to her.

"Greetings and honor to our brave travelers. I hope that after rest and refreshment they will tell us about their adventures, then let us visit their miraculous ship."

Tobio was about to answer when there appeared in the doorway, with his big, brown eyes opened wide and aware of the attention he'd just attracted, Tobio's little brother, Pierre. While the boy stared in awe, Tobio, never thinking that he'd see his little brother looking so calm, ran up and hugged him.

The boy declared, "We've just arrived in the secta-phore. We still live with your mentor Sirius. He came back from the Great Spirit. He's the one who brought us here."

Impatiently, Tobio ran to meet his family. They were all radiantly healthy. His mother was merry, his father tan with calm, bright eyes, his sister, oh goodness, looked like a fay and the sorcerer Sirius, so noble, was watching him with smiling eyes.

A thousand dragons, the most harrowing dangers couldn't have made Tobio's heart beat any faster.

He gasped, "How good it is, after a long trip, to see your loved ones."

Then he remembered Seggor, afraid that he might be feeling lonely. He was about to call for him when he saw him gaping in wonder at his sister.

He thought, "Seggor certainly has an endless supply of passion. I don't have to worry about him for the moment. He won't get bored."

At the end of the meal the dwarves and pixies marched in ceremoniously, one behind the other, carrying in their arms huge piles of sweets on pearl platters. The fays especially enjoyed themselves and Tomaton felt his legs wobbling when the queen declared:

"I've never tasted such delicious treats. There's obviously a secret. Congratulations to the creator of these culinary masterpieces!"

It was the opportunity for Tobio to describe Dreamland and start to tell his tale. He talked excitedly about the leaders of this new world. The fays tried to imagine their friend as queen, and the sorcerers smiled at the thought of the passionate king Elegant would make. The dwarves, who loved stories, reveled in this glorious gift in utter silence and almost forgetting to breath. But then they huffed and puffed when Tobio described the cruel lords and they got scared when he told of the black star.

Sorcerer Sirius was contemplating his ward and at the mention of Saturn a little glimmer of interest flashed in his eyes.

Tobio finally stopped talking and loud applause broke out. The King of the Fays walked up to him and pinned a big diamond star on his chest, exactly like the one he himself wore.

He said, "This is the highest distinction Jupiter can offer you. Until today, only your mentor Sirius has received one. His student has proved himself worthy."

Tobio had to wait a long time for the clapping to die down. Then he responded, "Thank you, Majesty, for the great honor you pay me. But please let me share it with my friend Astrobus, the clever inventor of the Tobiophyllox."

"Oh, we haven't forgotten him and my new friend Ramines X will tell you all about it. But I think your friend wants to say something."

Astonished, Tobio saw Seggor stand up. Throwing back his proud shoulders, holding his magnificent head high, simple and noble, he said, "Although the tale that Tobio has told you of his adventures is true and accurate, it's not complete. Allow me to finish it."

And to Tobio's great bewilderment, Seggor told them about how his friend had saved his life.

After this anecdote, the fays shouted while throwing their flowers, "Long live Tobio! Long live Seggor!"

When their excitement calmed down, the somber Wizard King took the floor.

"It's time, I believe, to satisfy the curiosity of the brave adventurers with respect to me. From the astonished eyes of your detective and from the furrowed brow of your scientist on seeing me present here, I understand that, for them, I'm still the fox in the hen house. I'd like to reassure them, to tell them that peace reigns from now on between our peoples ever since the King of the Fays granted me the fortress Hauroc."

Astrobus looked heartbroken at this friend Tobio who was so shocked he had to swallow several times before managing to stammer, "It can't be true."

The King of the Fays was so heavyhearted that he couldn't find anything to say.

Sirius stepped forward. "Tobio, Seggor and you, Astrobus, come with us, with Ramines X and me, to the fortress. I'll explain everything on the way."

His mentor seemed to accept the situation as natural. Tobio calmed down and followed them with his friends.

"I... I..." Astrobus stuttered furiously when he saw Ramines X climb into Hup! Hup!.

"Come on, Astrobus," Tobio consoled, "let's wait for my mentor to tell us what's going on. Climb in."

But the dwarf turned his back to the sectaphore where his young friends had already sat down and went to sit behind the wheel of Hup! Hup!, forcing Ramines X to move over.

Everyone who was there had a big laugh when the chubby vehicle shot off, lurching and tottering violently.

But Ramines X didn't lose his cool. He simply said, "Oh, what an impulsive pilot you are, my friend."

As he was about to bark a mean reply, Astrobus saw a huge flat building lying next to Hauroc.

"That's the laboratory I got built for you," Ramines X said.

"For me?"

"Of course. And it goes without saying that I'll be working with you."

"Oh really!" the dwarf responded defiantly. And to prove his displeasure he landed so hard that he almost crashed into the sectaphore.

Tobio yelled, "Hey, Astrobus, watch out! This is no time for acrobatics!"

But the dwarf, gaping at Hauroc, didn't answer. The door had changed place and seemed to be watching the new arrivals with amusement from the second story.

Ramines X put a key into a hidden hole in the wall and the spectators gawked as the door opened from top to bottom, extended its length and formed a bridge down to the feet of the visitors.

"A little, personal invention," the Wizard King rubbed his hands gleefully.

"You see," Sirius smiled slyly, "our friend Ramines X has become a passionate inventor. War and squabbling no longer interest him since he's so busy turning Hauroc into the most fantastic fortress."

If the Wizard K ing had heard this, he wouldhave turned red with pleasure, but he was taking Astrobus, whose great weakness was always curiosity, to the laboratory.

Tobio was forcing himself to keep a straight face. "This is no doubt all a result of your diplomatic activity, mentor?"

"I won't deny it," Sirius gave him a conspiratorial wink. "You'll excuse me, I hope, but a thousand years of peace for a whole planet deserves a fortress!"

"For sure," Tobio agreed. "But tell me, mentor, what do the wizards think of this new hobby of their king?"

"Ha, ha, what do they think? There's no way to know because we don't see one of them on the streets anymore. The invention bug has contaminated all of them! They're working, shut up in their castles, just working away, trying to outdo each other with extraordinary novelties. Come on, you can see for yourself the results of the epidemic."

Sirius marched off, with the two inquisitive young men in his wake, towards the wizards' dwellings.

The first they saw belonged to Ramines X' close friend. It was very simple, looking like a huge tower.

"At least this one didn't change his house," Tobio commented.

"Really," the sorcerer started laughing when he saw the indescribable looks on the faces of his two companions.

Pushing open the gate had set off an ingenious system that started shaking the roof, which rose and fell under the effect of steam like a pot of boiling water.

"But mentor, that's not an invention, that's madness," Tobio exclaimed.

"Or a trick or whatever, it doesn't matter, my boy. We're not complaining since the wizards are kept busy and we can live in peace."

"And to think I travel to other planets to discover the extraordinary…" Tobio muttered.

CHAPTER X
Earth

Happy to be with his family, Tobio stopped thinking about leaving. As for Seggor, he was living in perpetual delight since his friend's sister was in charge of showing him around the country. Astrobus, however, who found the constant advice and orders of Ramines X insufferable in the laboratory, was becoming gloomy.

One day Tobio caught him staring at the sky and sighing. "Missing our travels, Astrobus?"

"Um, yes, in any case mine."

"What do you mean yours?"

"Well, Earth."

Tobio felt guilty and cried out, "It's a good thing you reminded me. Nobody will ever say I didn't keep my word. Come on, old dwarf, put a smile on and get ready. We're leaving tomorrow after the welcome."

Astrobus blushed with joy and after stammering his thanks to his friend he went hopping away like a bird to announce the good news to Tomaton.

"Oh, my pixies," the chef shouted when he heard the news, "to the pastries, to the pastries, and you, dwarves, to the nectar! We'll have to fill up the pantry of the Tobiophyllox all night long. I have no idea what we'll find on Earth, but whatever it is my boarders have to be fed."

Tobio's sister remarked how their first expedition had been prepared with the Dream Fay on board, and, without any explanation, she decided to replace her for this one. Seggor thought it an excellent idea so Tobio dared not make any objections.

The next day, after the welcome, as the three friends were arriving with the whole family at the Tobiophyllox, they all had a good laugh on seeing Tomaton planted in the doorway, waiting for them, with all his utensils hanging from his apron, wearing a white chef's hat and his flour-caked hands on his hips. Astrobus' big head was stuck in the fluid tank.

Tobio asked Sirius, "Don't you want to come with us, mentor?"

"No, my boy, I'm not needed there but maybe your parents would like to see their home planet again?"

"With all of the worries and problems? No thanks," Tobio said.

With one final, tender look at his family, he bowed to the King, waved to the crowd gathering around and scampered up the ladder.

As he was about to close the door, he heard his brother's voice shouting, "Don't forget to bring me back some books!"

"Funny kid. Books and sweets make him happy," Tomaton said as he waved farewell with a big, shiny spoon.

The Tobiophyllox had never risen or shot off into space as fast as it did this time. Astrobus was obviously very excited to see Earth.

During the whole trip, Seggor and Tobio's sister were at the telescope almost all the time, which had been the former refuge of Elegant and the Dream Fay. Together they admired Venus wrapped in its rosy atmosphere, bright Mercury, and the Moon that, contrary to what the poets say of its silvery reflections, looked golden. Seggor, who had never seen the Sun so close, knew that it was the King of the Heavens.

Passing through the Milky Way made Astrobus so worried that he was sweating. He didn't know how to pilot his ship in the starry bath and ended up closing his eyes and waiting for the collision. When nothing happened he ran joyfully to find his friend who was furrowing his brow as he searched space through the telescope.

"What a voyage, Tobio!" he cried out. "Did you see where we just flew through?"

"Yes, yes," Tobio answered distractedly. "Hurray! Earth is in sight!"

"Magnificent!" the dwarf exclaimed. "Let me see and you take control of the ship since you know the planet. I hope we'll land in your country."

"That won't be easy, Astrobus. Right now we're nearing an ocean. Let out a little fluid until we've passed it. Oh, what a pain! Look how the night is about to fall over this part of the globe!"

In fact, it was already dark when the ship settled at a comfortable speed around 10,000 feet over the land.

"Oh, Tobio, look," Astrobus was pointing at the flying vehicles whizzing by them.

Tobio didn't have time to realize what was happening. The Tobiophyllox was bounced around like a ball being kicked and loud noises exploded along with flashes of light.

"They're firing at us!" Tobio's sister shouted with tears in her eyes.

Tobio was the picture of astonishment. He seriously wondered if the inhabitants of this planet had gone crazy. Then he grabbed a pair of binoculars and scrutinized what was happening outside their protective walls.

As the ship was regaining its balance, he suddenly cried out, "I've got it. Come over and I'll explain. The men are at war. We got here in the middle of an air battle.

Each side thinks their enemy built a new machine. When the first pilots saw that our ship is invulnerable to their bullets, they were frightened away. Their enemies had the same reaction and in fifteen minutes all the newspapers on Earth will be reporting the appearance of a fantastic new aircraft. Ha, Astrobus, your invention is even better than you imagined. Luckily, or else we'd have been shot down and killed."

"But... but, Tobio, you didn't tell me your fellow men were mean. We've haven't been received like this on any other star."

"No, Astrobus, they're not mean, but unhappy. See, among them, scattered around, are monsters who plan and organize wars and send millions of men they've never seen to kill one another."

"Are there really a lot of these monsters and are they really so powerful?"

"No, just a few dozen in certain nations. They only have two powers: evil and money."

"Um, excuse me, Tobio, I wouldn't want to be impolite but I don't understand very well how millions of men could submit themselves, to their own harm, to a few dozen others. Are they really so stupid?"

"Unhappy, I said, Astrobus. But the night is fading. Heavens, what's that down there burning? A whole village with women, children, elderly and sick. What an atrocity! How could they? Faster, Astrobus, let's get out of here!"

Saddened, his head buried in his hands, Tobio wept. His planet all darkened with hatred, streaming with tears and blood amidst the splendor of the universe.

Astrobus suddenly cried out, "Oh, Tobio, how beautiful it is!"

238

"Beautiful?" Tobio wiped his eyes and nose with his shirtsleeve. He only had to take one look and he jumped up and started dancing in circles.

"My country! Switzerland! Living in peace! There are the white peaks that are turned pink by the kiss of dawn and that's an alpine pasture covered in rhododendrons. Oh, Astrobus, quickly, let's land."

Soon afterward the whole troop was sitting on the bank of a fresh, babbling spring. In the distance cowbells were tinkling. On a slope, at the entrance to its home, a marmot was standing sentinel, whistling to the colony that there were strangers. All of a sudden, in the pure morning air, a loud, melodious sound rang out.

Seggor and Astrobus both yelped, "Oh!"

"A horn," Tobio breathed deeply, "giving thanks that will fill the heavens."

Tomaton came running up, "Did you hear that? The mountains are singing."

"Oh, Tobio, we have to stay here," Astrobus said. "I've never felt my mind so sparkling. I think I could finish the machine I've got planned without adding another lump to my head."

"Ha, ha, ha, my poor Astrobus, where would get the necessary equipment? And are you going to set up your lab on this peak? Are you going to store your inventions in that rocky crevice?"

"What a great idea! Bravo! Yes, that's where we'll hide it—the machine to guarantee Peace on Earth."

"Say that again! Is it really possible? I'd work day and night, I'd give my life to achieve such a thing! But we're talking fairy tales. We don't even have a laboratory."

"If you weren't so busy on Jupiter, Tobio, you would've noticed that I set one up in the Tobiophyllox. I couldn't stand working with Ramines X so I hunkered down in the ship. Do you know what I found?"

"No."

"That thoughts are a stronger force than solar energy or electricity. I built a device capable of receiving them, then sending them back as powerful waves."

"But Astrobus, how can we use that for Peace?"

"Well, we'll adjust it so that it captures only bad thoughts. Suppose one of your monsters, to satisfy his passions or his outrageous ambition, wants to start a war. His evil-infested thoughts will come to my machine and, given their diabolical nature, they'll be transformed into lethal fluid."

"You mean death rays, Astrobus? And who will we aim them at?"

"They'll return automatically to the sender, to the evil thinker who will be killed on the spot."

"Marvelous, Astrobus! So, evil will destroy itself."

Finally understanding how valuable this invention was, Tobio started jumping with joy and showering Astrobus with compliments.

"Wonderful little creature! You'll be the savior of my planet. They'll celebrate your name everywhere. Your portrait will hang in all the classrooms and they'll build monuments…"

"Stop, Tobio! Please be quiet. Our invention has to remain a secret. When it's working, we'll go back to Jupiter to celebrate the engagement of these two who…"

Tobio looked at his sister and Seggor picking Alpine roses. He shook his head, "What kids! Let them be happy. Say, Astrobus, do you distrust the thanks from humans so much that you want to run away?"

"Um, it's not that. But you know, your story of a few dozen against millions…"

"What do you mean?"

"Um, nothing, Tobio. I think that a dwarf's brain will never be able to understand the problems of humans."

Tobio contemplated the dwarf, then after a moment of reflection he said, "I believe the opposite, that your dwarf's brain understands perfectly why humans are unhappy."

Then thinking again about the marvelous machine for peace, Tobio jumped up and cried out, "Let's go, Astrobus, let's get to work."